Journey of Faith:
FAMILIAR
STRANGERS

Uncle Johnny,
 Enjoy the ~~book~~!
 Donna C. Stephens

Uncle Johnny:
Donna C. Stephens

Journey of Faith:
FAMILIAR STRANGERS

Donna Connelly Stephens

TATE PUBLISHING & Enterprises

Published by Tate Publishing & Enterprises, LLC
127 E. Trade Center Terrace | Mustang, Oklahoma 73064 USA
1.888.361.9473 | www.tatepublishing.com

Tate Publishing is committed to excellence in the publishing industry. The company reflects the philosophy established by the founders, based on Psalm 68:11,
"The Lord gave the word and great was the company of those who published it."

Book design copyright © 2009 by Tate Publishing, LLC. All rights reserved.
Cover design by Lance Waldrop
Interior design by Stefanie Rooney

Published in the United States of America

ISBN: 978-1-60696-144-5
1. Fiction, Christian, Romance
2. Fiction, Romance, Western
09.01.08

Dedication

To my husband, Gary, for his patience
as we were out on our boat,
and I would write while he fished.

Acknowledgments

Thank you to the family at Tate Publishing.

To those who critiqued my book:

Karen Prince, my gospel singing partner
Shane Prince, a lawyer in Philadelphia
Laura Boswell, a professor at Marshall University
Bill McKnaught, former professor
at a Michigan University
And the members of Appalachian Heritage Writers

Foreword

I have known Donna Connelly Stephens for several years. She is a member of Appalachian Heritage Writers in Carter County, Kentucky. She is an adept writer and has won several awards in our local writing contests. Donna is a fine Christian, active in the Salem Missionary Baptist Church where she is a member.

In this book, her first, she has emptied her heart, soul, mind, and strength to bring you words that build faith and character. My wish for all readers is that they will find nourishment for their souls, and that they will have become better, stronger individuals after reading the book. My hope is that the hearts of many readers will be touched by the contents of this book.

Lois Bays - Author of *God's Rare Gift*
and *They Lit Their Lamps for Us*

Chapter One

> *And we know that all things work together for good to them that love God...*
>
> Romans 8:28a

Rebecca O'Brian sat quietly behind the solemn people gathered in the room as Jake Roberts, a respected Morgantown lawyer, read the will of the late Hester Malone.

"...And to my faithful servant and butler, Arthur Byron, who stood by me for over forty years, I bequeath the sum of one thousand dollars. To my housekeeper, Mary O'Toole, I bequeath one hundred dollars. To my maid, Annie Lewis, I bequeath fifty dollars."

The lawyer flipped a page and broke the silence that had settled in the room. Rebecca watched as his keen eyes scanned the group and halted on her face in the shadows at the back of the room.

"To my young friend and business partner, George Pickett, I bequeath my business, The Malone

Manufacturing Company, and the controlling stock. To my niece, Rebecca O'Brian, I bequeath my house, its furnishings, and the surrounding land. There is one condition, however." She held her breath as Mr. Roberts glanced again in her direction. He then reluctantly continued, "She must marry my business partner, George Pickett, within two months of my death."

She heard gasps as she slipped from the room, but not before she observed the smug expression on George's face as he looked around the room.

Rebecca watched from the shadows of the landing as the group dispersed. She observed Mr. Roberts watch as George strutted around the room, his effeminate ways obvious in his every move. Her tender heart went out to the lawyer as with a weary sigh he gathered his papers and stepped into the foyer. Arthur stood respectfully at his post. He opened the door, but gave the lawyer a cold, hard stare. Mr. Roberts paused on the threshold. His voice carried into the shadows on the landing.

"I only fulfill my clients' wishes, Arthur, even if I don't always agree with them."

Arthur's expression softened. "I understand, Mr. Roberts. Have a good day, sir."

———◆◆———

Rebecca paced back and forth across the imported wool carpet of the library. The events of the day had created a whirlwind of turmoil in her mind. She stopped to gaze out the rain-streaked window. "I won't marry that evil man!" she cried. *But what will I do? I don't care about this house, but I don't know where to go.* As she watched the sun break through the rain-laden clouds, a peace enveloped her heart. *I will not sacrifice my life for fear of the future.* She turned from the window with a new resolve, then hurried upstairs to her room and knelt by her bed to pray.

God, I know my life is in your hands and I will accept whatever you will in my life. I leave it all to you, God, but please, show me what you want me to do. She poured her heart out to God, then stood and took a deep breath. She was now ready to face the day.

With lighthearted steps she descended the stairs. She located Arthur watering lush ferns that graced the verandah off the dining room.

"Arthur, will you bring the carriage around at six o'clock. I'm going to the Rileys' for dinner tonight."

"Yes, Miss Becky," he said, giving her a warm smile.

She returned his smile and gave thanks in her heart for her dear friend. Over the past two years, she had developed a close bond with the impeccable, English-born butler. He emitted an aura of great inner strength and trusted God in all matters.

"I hope the neighbors won't think I'm being disrespectful by going out so soon after the funeral, but the Rileys were Mother's best friends and I'm in need of a shoulder to lean on."

"You go and have a good time, Miss Becky. Don't worry about the neighbors. I didn't see them rush to your side when your Uncle Hess was on his deathbed."

"Thanks, Arthur."

Later, she chose from her wardrobe an emerald green, satin dress. She needed to dress up, to give her spirits a lift. She knew the dress was becoming paired with her red-gold hair and fair skin. She wore it over a hip-pad bustle that forced it to hang straight down in front and sweep wide in back. Its high collar and large puff sleeves accentuated her small waist. She arranged her hair in an upswept style, but allowed a few red-gold tendrils to curl on her forehead and about her ears, then adorned it with an enameled comb that had belonged to her grandmother. A small, heart-shaped gold locket completed the ensemble.

As they rode across town to the Rileys', Rebecca and Arthur discussed the will. His obvious disgust revealed what he thought of his employer's manipulative tactics.

"Miss Becky, you must do what you think is best, but remember, marriage is a lifelong commitment. I hope you will give it plenty of thought before you make a decision. The Bible says 'be ye not unequally yoked together with unbelievers.' Pickett shows no evidence of being a child of God."

"Oh, Arthur, the only decision I'm concerned about is this: do I know what God wants me to do? I simply refuse to marry that wicked man. He's so conceited; why, I haven't even given a thought to accepting his proposal. As he left the house today, he remarked, 'I'll be away on business for about three weeks, but I expect you to be ready for the wedding when I return.' He thinks I'm as greedy as he is! I won't marry him just to satisfy my uncle's fantasy.

"Dear friend," she sighed, patting his aged hand, "just pray with me that I will know what God wants me to do and accept what he has planned for my future."

It's good we do not know the future, she thought. *We'd be tempted to turn and run the other way. We have to depend on him for daily needs, and I know he'll work it out for my good. I must entrust the unknown future to the all-knowing God.*

———◆———

The modest house on Elm Street had been the Riley home since their children had been small. It was a pleasant home, simply furnished and neat as a pin. Mr. Riley owned a general merchandise store where he made a modest, but adequate income on which he and Agnes had raised eight children, all now married and living in different parts of the state.

Arthur helped Rebecca from the carriage as Agnes rushed through the doorway and enfolded Rebecca in her ample arms.

"Child, I'm so glad you decided to come." Rebecca graciously accepted the peck on her cheek. "Our son Edmund and his wife just came, and they brought a friend with them, a Matthew Holt. He has just returned from out West, and he's going to tell us all about his trip." Excitement shone in her eyes.

Before Rebecca could reply, Mrs. Riley rambled

on with other details as they entered the cool interior of the foyer. The other guests were gathered in the dining room, and soon everyone was seated around the table.

"Pastor, will you ask the blessing on the food?" asked William Riley as he stood at the head of the table.

The preacher bowed his head in reverent prayer. "Our Heavenly Father, we humbly bow in thy presence, asking forgiveness for all our sins. Lord, we thank you for this food we are about to partake of and for the one that so willingly prepared it. Be with the Rileys and the other guests as they go about their daily lives, and may we all put you first in all things. Amen."

Agnes placed a platter heaped with fried chicken in the center of the large table along with a variety of vegetables and big, fluffy buttermilk biscuits. The delicious aroma permeated the room. Mr. Holt, who was talented in the art of storytelling, kept everyone's interest with his tales of the West and how the new state of Colorado had grown.

"My younger brother, Josh, has a beautiful ranch in the Platte Valley. I've purchased a tract of land from him on the northern section of his spread. I'll be leaving next spring with my family. Now that the railroad has been built and the cattle can be shipped to market by rail, more people have moved into the territory. The land can support large herds, and there is plenty of water from the snow-capped Rocky Mountains. The aspens grow abundantly, providing an oasis of shelter for a homestead. Many of the settlers have become farmers after discovering how rich and fertile the land is."

The tales entranced Rebecca. Restlessness pervaded her as she imagined a move west and a new life in the rugged wilderness.

"I asked Josh if he wanted anything from back east. He said, 'If you can find one that can withstand this country and not be too much trouble,' Matt drawled, in imitation of his brother, 'you might bring me back a wife.'"

Matthew's large frame shook with laughter. "Knowing how Josh is set in his ways and his seeming disinterest in women, he would be fit to be tied if I turned up with a bride. But," he said with a dramatic sigh, "he made sure before I left that I knew he was joking. I'm almost tempted," a mischievous grin brightened his face, "to show up with one anyway."

The rest of the conversation during the meal was lost on Rebecca as she thought about Matt's last statement. She'd never had time to be courted in the last few years. Those who had showed an interest soon looked to others, since she had devoted herself to the care of the sick members of her family. Almost all the respectable young men had already married and started families, although none of them had been of real interest to her anyway. But now, faced with no home or position, and the urgency to escape the overbearing George Pickett's grasp, the thought of a move west tempted her.

I could get a teaching position, she reasoned, *but is*

it my future to spend the rest of my life teaching other people's children? If I take the money Father kept back for my education, I could go out West and never worry about George locating me.

The desire for a home, husband, and family swelled deep in her heart and mind. She believed that a woman's place was in the home. This was God's plan and he would provide. But she couldn't believe he had planted in her mind the idea to go West and marry a complete stranger. She had no idea what kind of man this Joshua Holt was, but the thought persisted and challenged her to consider the option. Matthew Holt sure had the highest opinion of his brother, but sometimes a person's love for his family could blind him to their faults.

Later, fellowship time came to a close and the guests prepared to leave. Rebecca waited on the porch for Arthur to bring the carriage around. Matthew stepped out and started a conversation with her. He again mentioned his brother and before she had time to consider her words, she asked: "Mr. Holt, is your brother a Christian man?"

"Yes, but I'm afraid he's not as close to the Lord as he used to be. There are very few sound churches out West. Why do you ask?"

"Well," she replied, with a slight quiver in her voice. "I'm suddenly on my own with no family, and I thought I might move out west. If you should decide your brother was really serious about a wife, I'd consider making the move. That is, if you think I would be appropriate and be what he would want in a wife.

I'm not beautiful, but I am a good hard worker and real strong and healthy. I just thought I'd mention it to you,—oh, there comes Arthur. Have a nice evening, Mr. Holt," she said breathlessly as she hurried down the flagstone walk and out the white picket gate. Behind her she left a surprised and bemused man.

"Can you believe that little lady," Matt murmured, as he thought about what had just transpired. "I believe she'd really do it. And she would be just what Josh needs."

He'd silently admired Rebecca all evening as she drank in the tales of the West with wide, eager eyes. He was sure she didn't realize how untamed the country was. The fact that she wouldn't offer herself to a man who wasn't a Christian was a great attribute to her character.

I wonder what Josh would say if she came out with us in the spring? A grin appeared at the thought as he turned to go in the house. *I just might give her a visit before I head toward home.*

Chapter Two

> *I will instruct thee and teach thee in the way which thou shalt go: I will guide thee with mine eye.*
>
> Psalm 32:8

The letters Matthew had received from his brother over the last couple of years sang Colorado's praises and had persuaded him to visit this past spring. He also fell in love with the beautiful mountains and valleys. He was prepared to return to Pittsburgh to sell his business and make arrangements for the move in a few months, but before he boarded the train for home, he decided to pay a visit to Rebecca O'Brian. He wondered if she had been serious about going west.

He stood before the stately, two-story brick home. By the appearance of this home, he surmised that she was used to the finer things in life. The door opened and a man with slightly stooped shoulders and silvery gray hair appeared.

"May I help you?" Arthur inquired, as he tried to place the young man.

"Could I please speak with Miss O'Brian? My name is Matthew Holt."

Arthur stepped back into the foyer to allow him entry and then led him into the parlor. He then hurried toward the kitchen where Rebecca was baking cookies for the church bazaar.

"Miss Becky, there's a Matthew Holt in the parlor who wishes to speak with you." A look of panic appeared briefly in her eyes.

Rebecca hurriedly removed her white apron. With hands that shook slightly, she smoothed back her hair and tucked in a few stray wisps. She paused before the parlor door, took a deep breath, and put on a smile. Matthew's warm smile quickly set her at ease and she greeted him curiously.

"Miss O'Brian, I was wondering if you had given any more thought to what we discussed the other night. If you are still planning to move west, I thought I'd write my brother and tell him you were coming out with us in the spring."

"Oh, but I can't wait that long!" she exclaimed. Matthew raised an eyebrow in question. "I mean," she quickly added, "I have to be moved out of this house in two weeks and I have no place to go. I hope to start west early next week. Do you think he would mind if I came on out?"

"Rebecca, I must be sure you know what you are facing. Josh doesn't have a fine house like this, only a hewn log house. It's a roomy house compared to a lot of homes out there. The previous owners had a large family. But, it's very rustic and Josh isn't the best housekeeper."

"I'm not afraid of work, Mr. Holt," she interrupted, "and I would feel more at home in a cabin than I do in this house. I have lived and worked here for two years. Before that, my mother and I lived in the humblest of homes with few conveniences. My uncle has placed conditions in his will that I can't honor, so I have to leave. I won't marry the ungodly man he chose for me before he died. I must get away before this man returns to town. I'm afraid he may try to follow me, so, I don't want him to discover where I have gone. If it's not possible for me to go out to Colorado, then I must go on to California … or Oregon. I have money for my train ticket, so I won't be a financial burden."

She was near tears, and Matt admired her for the control she showed and the determination to go forward with her plans. "All right, Rebecca. I believe this is the right thing to do … for Josh's sake as well as your own. I'll send Josh a wire and tell him his bride is on her way." A chuckle escaped as he thought of Josh's reaction. "When you arrive in Denver, send him a wire to let him know when you will arrive in Longmont, and he will be there to meet you. I hope you will be happy there. The Platte Valley is a beautiful region. I know you will make Josh a wonderful wife. Hannah and I will arrive with our family next spring, and I'm sure you'll become the best of friends. My Hannah is a real talker and she'll need another woman to talk to and confide in." He nervously ran his fingers through his curly brown hair, then put on his gray felt hat. "You be very careful on your way out. There are some rough characters out there."

Arthur escorted him to the door as Rebecca hurried upstairs. Closing her bedroom door, she fell to her knees by her bedside.

"Oh, God," she whispered, "Have I gone too far? I can't believe this is the way you are leading me. But I trust in you, Lord, and I know if this weren't your will it would not have worked out. Lord, please continue to guide me, and let Josh be a kind man who will respect me. And Lord, I pray we can always serve you together. Be with me the next few days as I get ready, and guide me in making all the right decisions."

She walked to her window, pulled aside the heavy damask curtains, and gazed out over the meticulously groomed rose garden. Tears begin to fill the green eyes.

"Oh, Mother," she cried, "I miss you so. I wish you were here to guide me with your wisdom…to comfort me, to hold me in your arms once again as you did when I was a child. I wish you could meet this man who will soon become my husband. Just to know you approve of him would be all the assurance I need." She stood and pondered the future, and planned what needed to be done before she would be ready for this step of faith.

Chapter Three

> *Better is a dry morsel, and quietness therewith, than an house full of sacrifices with strife.*
>
> Proverbs 17:1

Rebecca arose early the next morning with avid determination. She needed to move swiftly. First, she wanted to tell Arthur of her decision. *I'll miss that dear man.* She located him in the breakfast room off the kitchen where he had just finished some coffee and scones. As she entered the room, he arose to go about his duties.

"Arthur, I need to talk to you. Will you stay a moment, please?" He returned to his chair as she poured him another cup of coffee. "I want to tell you of my decision and ask for your help. I don't want anyone else to know of my plans so they won't get back to George. I have confidence you will keep my plans to yourself."

She paused and took a deep breath. "I'm leaving in a few days to go out West. I've given much thought and prayer to this move, and I feel it's what God has planned for me." She paused again and looked into his keen gray eyes. She saw the look of question, but continued. "I'm going to Colorado to marry Joshua Holt."

"Humph. And who, may I ask, is this Joshua Holt? I thought his name was Matthew! And just what do you know about this man."

"Arthur," she pleaded, "please listen to me. The man that was here yesterday was Matthew Holt. Joshua is his brother, and Mr. Holt assures me he is a fine Christian man. I can't believe I am doing this either, but it seems to be the way God is leading me. I know if I trust him, I can't go wrong."

"Well, when do we leave?"

"What do you mean by 'we'?" she exclaimed as she looked into his gray eyes and saw a faint twinkle.

"You don't think I would actually let you start out to that wild country without someone to protect you. And, I'm certainly not staying here to work for that Mr. Pickett, so I might as well go with you."

"But, Arthur, I'm afraid there won't be jobs for butlers out there! It's a new country and people don't have homes that require that kind of work."

"Well, I rode horses in England and I'm sure I can be a 'cowpoke' as well as the next fellow."

She smiled. "Arthur, Arthur. Chasing foxes over the glen and herding cattle aren't exactly the same thing."

"Well, I'm going anyway. You can just pretend

you don't know me, but I'll be close by to protect you. So, when do we leave?"

With a smile and quick hug for her dear friend, she replied, "I don't want to leave from here in town and allow George to be able to trace where I've gone. I believe George will do anything to continue to make my life miserable. So ... could you go to Fairmont and buy tickets for us? While you're gone, I'll get my belongings packed. I looked over my copy of the will, and Uncle Hess did say that if I didn't marry George, I could have my mother's belongings and a few things to set up housekeeping, although I'm sure he never expected me to make this decision. When you return, you can get a couple of trunks from the attic. Are Mary and Annie staying to work for George?"

"No, Miss Becky. In fact, Mary has a fine prospect for a job, but she's waiting to see what you are going to do. If you were staying, she wouldn't leave you."

"Do you think we can get the house closed up in three days? That way neither George nor Mr. Roberts can complain about the house being left in servants' hands. We can mail the key to Mr. Roberts as we leave town."

"I'll assign Mary and Annie their duties before I leave this morning."

She suspected he had suddenly become excited about the way his life was about to change. "They only need to know that you won't be staying here," he continued as he hurried toward the kitchen, and soon Mary arrived with her coffee and scones.

Rebecca quickly ate breakfast and then disappeared into her room. She took her dresses from the armoire, folded them, and placed them on the bed. She folded the cherished quilts she and her mother had quilted together before she had become ill. There was a double Wedding Ring done in pastels that was her favorite, a red and white Sawtooth Star, a Drunkard's Path set up in blues and a couple of simple Nine Patches. Three sets of linens, some crocheted dresser scarves her mother had made, and a picture of her parents on their wedding day. All the things that had belonged to her mother were in her suite of rooms. She yearned to sit and reminisce as she gathered up the few treasures from her childhood, but she suppressed the desire and soon had everything ready to place in the trunks.

She glanced around the near empty room and then hurried to the kitchen where Annie and Mary were busy with their duties.

"Annie, don't we have some pans and skillets somewhere that aren't used now?"

Annie stepped into the big walk-in pantry and carried out a wooden crate holding a mixture of cookware. "This be what you were thinkin' 'bout?" she asked.

"Yes, that's just what I need. Just set it over by the door and Arthur will take care of it when he returns."

She then showed Rebecca some silverware that

had been discarded when Mr. Malone had purchased the exquisite new silver. "Ain't no use to keep these around if you could use 'em." Along with the silver, a set of dishes with delicate yellow and blue flowers scattered around the rim was set out. They reminded Rebecca of the times she would slip in and have a meal in the kitchen, eat from these plates, and drink Mary's hot tea from the dainty cups. Mary, who knew how she admired the dishes, packed them securely and placed them in a wooden barrel.

Lunch was a quiet affair, and soon Rebecca headed to the bank where she planned to withdraw her savings, including what her father had left for her education. A spring rain earlier in the day had left the air cool and damp, which made the walk uncomfortable. She was careful as she picked her way around the mud holes and soon reached the boardwalk. She briskly approached the bank, the heels of her black boots echoing on the wooden boards.

When her business at the bank was completed, she crossed over to Mr. Riley's store. As she entered the dim interior of the store, he greeted her warmly.

"Good morning, Miss O'Brian. What can I do for you today?"

She glanced over the well-stocked shelves. "I guess I need to look at that new material you got in last week," she grinned.

"I'd say so," he laughed. "Just look all you want."

Since she didn't know how far it would be from the ranch to a town, she decided on a couple lengths of material from the many colorful bolts of fabric, and some thread and buttons. She loved to cook, so she chose an assortment of herbs and spices. She smiled as she thought of Mary's advice that "The way to a man's heart is through his stomach."

———◆———

That night she wrote a letter to George and put her least favorite task behind her.

> *Mr. Pickett:*
>
> *I am sorry to leave while you are away, but I have secured a position and must leave at once. I hope you will understand and forgive me for going without giving you an answer in person, but you must know that I could never marry anyone whom I didn't love, or one who didn't love my Lord. I have taken the things that belonged to my mother and a few things for setting up housekeeping.*
>
> *I wish you much happiness in the future and hope you and your business continue to prosper. I pray that someday you will see the need of the Savior in your life.*
>
> *Sincerely,*
> *Rebecca O'Brian*

———◆———

Arthur, tired and dusty, returned from Fairmont around mid-afternoon the next day. He found that most of the work needed to close up the house had been finished. While Mary and Annie enjoyed a cup of tea, he searched for Rebecca and found her in the library.

Rebecca had been wandering through the rooms. They had been her home for the last two years, and although she didn't desire the many priceless possessions of her late uncle, she felt a sadness to leave the familiar rooms.

The evening sun had set in a cloudless sky, and the full moon now shone brightly. Everything inside the elegant home was cleaned and in its place. When Arthur entered the library she instructed him to have the stable boy bring Old Nell and the wagon around to the back of the house and help load up the trunks.

After a tearful good-bye, Mary and Annie went to their new positions and the doors were locked. A time in Rebecca's life was closed forever. They left town by the back roads to leave no witness to the direction of their departure.

On the outskirts of town was the cemetery where John and Susan O'Brian had been laid to rest. Arthur saw the sad look of yearning in Rebecca's eyes. He pulled the wagon off the road under a sprawling spruce tree that reached its branches out to protect the resting place of loved ones.

"Go and say your goodbyes, Missy. We may never return to the East." He climbed from the wagon, helped her down, and reached under the seat to pull out a rifle. "Just take your time, Miss Becky, and I'll keep watch."

With a smile of thankfulness to the understanding old man, she climbed the knoll to where her parents were buried. She knelt reverently and said goodbye to the best Christian parents a young girl could have been blessed with. They had taught her God's word from the cradle, and at the age of eleven she had accepted Christ as her savior. From that time, she had let him be her guide as she prayed about each decision in her life.

Chapter Four

> *I will lift up mine eyes unto the hills, from whence cometh my help.*
>
> Psalm 121:1

The days that followed were uneventful as they traveled out of West Virginia, across the farmlands of Ohio, Indiana, and Illinois, then into Missouri. In Kansas City they boarded the Kansas Pacific for the next step of their journey. The tree-shy landscape of Kansas made the journey seem endless. Most of the houses were made of sod, almost indistinguishable from the surrounding landscape. Some of the fence was made of lengths of limestone and stood like sentinels across the plains.

The train passed through Topeka, Fort Riley, and Selena, and finally pulled into Denver. Arthur checked the baggage at the station while Rebecca went to the telegraph office and sent a wire:

_To_   Joshua Holt, Longmont, Colorado

Have arrived in Denver

Arrive In Longmont Friday

Rebecca O'Brian

They crossed the dusty street where horse-drawn trolley cars, horses and riders, and buckboard wagons hustled about. They checked into the Denver Hotel. When Rebecca reached her room, the first thing on her agenda was a good, hot bath. The dust and cinders of the past few days had settled in her hair and clothes and left her feeling like a chimney sweep. As the housemaid poured in the last bucket of hot water and left the room, she locked the door, stepped out of her dusty clothes, and eased her travel-weary body into the hot, sudsy water with a sigh of contentment.

She washed her hair, then lathered all over with a lightly scented bar of soap. Her weary body relaxed, but thoughts of the coming days began to invade her mind. *What have I done? I haven't corresponded in any way with this Joshua Holt. He could very well have changed his mind about wanting a wife.* She hadn't stayed in Morgantown long enough to receive a reply to Matt's wire. Something had urged her to leave town as soon as possible. *Well, I'll know soon enough… as soon as I arrive on Friday.* A moment of prayer to God provided her with quiet reassurance that her life was in his hands. Any further worrisome thoughts were pushed from her mind.

She stepped from the cool water, wrapped a

towel around her hair, quickly dried, and slipped into a warm, pale blue robe. She toweled her red-gold hair, combed it until it began to dry and swirl in natural curls around her face, and flow down her back to below her waist. She then doffed the robe, slipped into soft undergarments and donned a light-gray, silky blouse. Over this she put on a gray suit with black velvet collar and cuffs. She moved across the room to a rocker by the window and rested her head against the cushioned back while she waited for Arthur's arrival.

The view from the window showed a hodge-podge of buildings down the main street that sported a variety of businesses. She had been pleasantly surprised to see the look of prosperity in this western town as she walked from the station.

When Arthur arrived, they walked down the street to a restaurant and enjoyed a pleasant meal. A young man in a black suit sat at the next table.

"Hasn't the Lord blessed us with a beautiful day," he remarked. He gave them both a warm, friendly smile.

"Er...yes he has," replied Arthur. He gave the man a once-over.

"You all live close by?" the stranger asked.

"No, we're just passing through." Arthur wasn't inclined to give any information to a stranger, no matter how respectable he looked.

"My name's Jonathan Smith. I'm a Baptist preacher from up north of here. I'm holding a meetin' outside of town the rest of the week. If you're in town for a few days, why don't you come out."

"That would be up to Miss O'Brian," said Arthur as he gave Rebecca a look of question.

"I'd like that," she smiled. "We haven't been to any services since we left back east."

He stood to leave and reached to shake Arthur's hand. "We'll be lookin' for you then. Good evenin' Sir, Ma'am."

They attended the services that evening, and Rebecca discovered the meaning of a 'fire and brimstone' sermon. She felt there were few who left the services that night who didn't think about their souls' destination. Brother Smith hailed from Virginia and was a spirit-filled young man whom God had blessed with a captive method of delivery that kept the attention of young and old alike. Rebecca didn't know then that their paths would one day cross again, or that he would eventually have a profound influence on her life.

The sun had dropped behind the mountains to the west as they started the final leg of their journey. The scenery changed little as the mountains rose in the distance and cast a shadow over the Platte Valley. The moon crept into the starry sky and lit a silvery path across the valley floor. Rebecca rested her head against the window and watched the mountain peaks in the distance. The verse from Psalm 121 came to her mind: *'I will lift up mine eyes unto the hills, from whence cometh my help'*.

Early the next morning they arrived in Longmont. As she started to step from the train onto the platform, she looked down into a bearded face with tobacco stains around his grinning mouth. She gasped, quickly drew back, and bumped into Arthur who stood close behind her.

"Move aside, sir," demanded Arthur to the uncouth man, "and let the lady pass."

"Jist wan'ed to help the pretty lady," he replied with a leer, but quickly backed away as he looked into Arthur's steely gray eyes.

Arthur promptly escorted her into the station and over to the clerk. "Has Joshua Holt been in this morning?" she asked timidly.

"No, Ma'am," he replied with a grin. "But just have a seat and I'm sure he'll be here soon. He's a man of his word."

She sat near the back of the waiting room and glanced about nervously while Arthur stood outside the door. A variety of men, mostly drifters, made their way into the room, some just to look at the pretty girl. Time crept by and she began to tremble as she pondered. *If these are the type of men this land produces, what have I gotten myself into?*

Chapter Five

> My son, hear the instruction of thy father, and forsake not the law of thy mother.
>
> Proverbs 1:8

Josh gazed down into the valley as a herd of cattle mingled aimlessly. The eighty or so herd of Black Angus was a new breed to this range. Three years earlier he had sold from the original herd of longhorn and begun to restock with this breed. They had proved to adapt much better to the newly fenced ranch land.

The One Bolt Ranch lay east of the divide, near the South Platte River where the grassy plains sloped up into the foothills of the Rockies and created an area that was ideal not only for cattle, but also for raising fruits and grains. He had planted an orchard near the ranch house and it flourished, producing a bounty of delicious fruit. In the lower valley he had planted his first wheat crop, and it would soon be ready to harvest.

Joshua Holt had been a tall lanky youth of twenty-one when he had come west in 1883. The hard work as a cowhand for the mighty cattle barons, then, as a ranch owner, had toughened him and filled out his six-foot, two-inch frame into a fine specimen of a man. His dark, wavy hair and drooping mustache, coupled with piercing blue eyes under heavy dark brows, gave him a menacing look. But his warm smile brought out his true personality of warmth and kindness.

His keen gaze drifted to the ranch house, and his thoughts wandered back to 1886. He had worked on this same ranch for John Daniels. The winter of 1886–1887 had proved to be one of the worst the cattlemen of Colorado had ever endured. More than half of all livestock had been killed, and most of the large cattle owners had never recovered from the blow. During one of the worst blizzards of that winter, John Daniels and three of his men had been lost in the storm and had perished. Daniels had left a wife and seven children at the mercy of the severe winter, with only a handful of men. Sarah Daniels had put Josh in charge, and he had managed to save close to eight hundred of the many thousands of cattle on the ranch.

When spring arrived, Sarah Daniels had vowed she would never endure another such winter. Josh eagerly offered to buy the ranch. She took her children and the bare necessities and moved back east to live with her brother. The loss of so many cattle during the severe winter caused the price of cattle to soar, and Josh had been able to sell many of the stock that remained and start to rebuild the ranch.

He leisurely rode toward the ranch house and entered the house where Dave, the ranch cook, stirred a huge kettle of stew over the open fireplace. Dave was a short, stocky Irishman with fiery red hair streaked with gray. He had been the cook and handyman since Josh had rescued him after he'd been waylaid in an alley, beaten and robbed. After he recovered at the ranch, he had stayed and become a faithful friend and confidant.

Josh poured a steaming cup of strong black coffee. He sat down at the kitchen table and leaned his elbows on the grimy surface as Charlie, the foreman, stomped through the doorway and headed for the coffeepot.

"I picked up the supplies for that fence on the north range, Boss," he drawled. "Got ya mail, too, and a tel'gram. Speck said it'd been there for days, but he couldn't find nobody comin' this way. Said he hoped it wasn't too 'portant. Well, I'd best get back to work," he said as he left the room with a chuckle.

Josh curiously opened the envelope and began to read as he took a sip of coffee. He turned ghastly pale, then spewed the coffee across the table. He stood suddenly; his chair upended and scooted across the floor.

"He didn't! I can't believe he'd do this to me! I'll wring his scrawny neck and hang 'im out to dry!" he exclaimed, as he rushed out the door.

Dave, not being able to contain his curiosity, picked up the discarded wire and read:

To. *Joshua Holt, Longmont, Colorado*
your bride Rebecca O'Brian arriving soon
God bless
Matt

"Whoopee!" Dave shouted. He danced around the huge room and sang:

> *No more cookin' for me!*
> *No more washin' for me.*
> *Got us a missy comin' to the ranch,*
> *No more cookin' for me.*

He quickly did a little Irish jig to finish his celebrating, then peeked out the window. On the west side of the house was a grove of trees beside a wandering stream. Here he had watched Josh work out many decisions in the past, and now, the thinkin' spot was getting a real workout.

———◆———

"What could Matt be thinking 'bout!" Josh mumbled. "I told him I didn't want no wife! She's probably some old school marm that nobody else would marry. If she's been raised back east, she won't be able to take this harsh land and the winter blizzards. Well, when she gets here and I explain to her what it's like, she'll hightail it right back east where she came from." As he stomped back and forth he muttered to himself. Charlie cautiously approached.

"Boss," he said as he tried to keep the smile from his face, "I forgot to give you this. Speck chased me down as I was leavin' town. I stuck it in my pocket and forgot all 'bout it," he explained innocently. He handed another wire to Josh and then scurried away.

Josh eagerly grabbed the envelope, sure that it would be from Matt telling him it was just a joke. But all eagerness faded as he read:

T. Joshua Holt, Longmont, Colorado
Have arrived in Denver
Arrive In Longmont Friday
Rebecca O'Brian

"Friday!" he exclaimed in dismay. "But that's tomorrow!"

"That's right, Boss," replied Charlie from a safe distance. "Tomorrow's Friday."

As Charlie turned the corner of the barn, out of range of Josh's ears, he doubled over in laughter at the expression he'd seen on Josh's face. *Matt better be glad he's not comin' 'til next spring,* he mused.

By evening every ranch hand had heard the news, but they dared not let their boss know. They watched him stomp around with a look much like a dark thundercloud. They didn't know how this situation had come about, but they enjoyed it to the fullest amongst themselves and in private.

<hr>

As Josh lay in bed that night, his mind and emotions in turmoil, he whispered, "Lord, I don't need a wife!" But as he looked around his room at the dust and cobwebs, the pile of untended clothes, the total disarray, he quickly added, "A housekeeper maybe, but not a wife!"

His thoughts drifted back to the loving and caring parents who had raised him, Matt and his younger sister, Catherine. When they had been youngsters, their mother would nightly take down the big Bible from the low shelf by the stone fireplace. She would sit in the big rocker beside the hearth and read to them from the Scriptures and expound on the word of God. They were taught to depend on God for guidance, to be faithful in serving him, and to obey his commandments to the best of their ability.

Joshua had brought this teaching west with him, but he had badly neglected the habit of attending church, as well as that of reading his Bible. Matt had mentioned that on his recent visit and caused him to contemplate his life the past few years. He missed the watchful and prayerful guidance of his dear Christian mother. He lay there and thought of his mother, who now lived with his sister in Pittsburgh, and a peace settled over him, and he seemed to hear her quiet voice. *Child, God knows what is best for you. All you have to do is listen, then obey. He will take care of the rest. Just trust and obey.*

Those words, spoken to him years before, seemed to be just what he needed at this time. His tired body relaxed, and he drifted off to sleep.

Chapter Six

Teach me to do thy will; for thou art my God...

Psalm 143:10a

Josh awoke the next morning with mixed feelings. Vanished were the good intentions from the previous night. He resented Matt for getting him into this situation and assumed a vengeful attitude. But guilt lay heavy as his plans for the day gave him the coward's way out of the situation. He didn't plan on showing up at the station.

He ignored Dave's questioning look when he entered the kitchen, and Dave kept quiet as Josh poured a cup of coffee, then drank deeply of the hot, steaming brew.

"I'm going to check on some horses this morning," Josh said evasively. "I should be back by dark."

He quickly downed the breakfast of eggs, ham, and hotcakes, washed them down with more hot coffee, then rushed out the door.

Dave watched from the window. Worry lines

creased his forehead as Josh rode out toward the mountains. "Now I wonder what he expects to happen to his little bride," he muttered. With a shake of his head, he shuffled out the back door to find Charlie.

"The boss say where he was going today?" he asked when he located Charlie in the barn grooming a golden Palomino mare that was due to foal soon.

"Yeah," Charlie frowned. "He said he was going up toward Ghost Canyon to check on that herd of wild horses he saw last month. I guess he ain't planning on meetin' the lady's train."

A shocked expression showed plainly on Dave's face. He stomped around the barn and took his anger out on anything in his path. "Why that stubborn, mule-headed coward. What's that little lady gonna think when he doesn't show up? She won't have no place to stay and she don't know nobody out here! I'm just gonna meet that train myself."

"Now, Dave, old man, you'd best just let it be." He watched Dave grab a bridle and head toward the corral. "Josh may come to his senses and head on into town. Remember, we ain't supposed to know nothin'."

"Well, he'd better show up," he replied as he hung the bridle back on the peg. "I'm sick and tired of cookin' for this bunch of hogs."

"I figured there was more to this show than worrin' 'bout the little lady." Charlie laughed as Dave stomped back toward the house.

◆

Josh let Duchess pick her own pace, giving him time to let his thoughts wander. He knew the train from Denver would be in around eight o'clock, and he was weighed down with guilt ... guilt that he had spurned Matt's judgment. "Duchess, old girl, I can't believe Matt's done this to us." The habit of talking to his horse was a way he had of putting his thoughts into words, especially when the thoughts were troublesome. "He should know I ain't gonna marry just any kind of woman."

He guided his horse into the rugged foothills. A small herd of horses still ran wild in the area. To pursue the herd had become a distracting challenge for him. The beauty of the rugged landscape was a balm to his weary soul. Still, he couldn't keep his thoughts off the woman waiting at the station.

"Girl, Matt's real smart when it comes to women." He patted Duchess's neck affectionately. "You know, she might be the very one we've been waiting for."

Oblivious to the dangers around him, he didn't notice the snake in the path, coiled and ready to strike. Duchess shied away, her back hooves floundering in the loose shale alongside the path, and soon horse and rider had slid into the gully below.

<hr/>

Arthur traipsed around the station and became more agitated as the afternoon sun dropped low on the horizon. *Where is that Holt fellow?* He glanced through the doorway. *I never should have let Miss Becky come.* She sat on the rough wooden bench with a dejected expression. Her troubled eyes searched each face that appeared.

Arthur approached the clerk. "I thought you said Joshua Holt was a man of his word." He glanced back at Rebecca with concern.

"Maybe he decided he didn't want no wife," Speck grinned.

"Well, she sure isn't going to wait for him any longer. Where's the best place to get a room?"

"If you're gonna be in town a while, you'd best go over to Molly's. She'll put you up, and feed you too."

Arthur quietly approached Rebecca and sat down beside her. "Miss Becky, let's get a room and something to eat, then we'll take the next step."

She raised her weary head and looked into Arthur's kind eyes. "He's not coming is he?" Tears pooled in her green eyes, turning them into misty lakes. "What will I do, Arthur?"

"Now, Miss Becky, don't give up yet. Something could have happened that kept him from showing. The clerk said we could get some rooms down the street at Molly's Boarding House."

Rebecca stood wearily. Arthur picked up her tote, placed his hand under her elbow, and escorted her from the station.

Molly's Boarding House bustled with activity. A heavyset woman in her fifties rushed around the dining room waiting on customers. She appeared flustered; her face flushed from the heat of the stove where she'd labored all afternoon. She threw her hands up in a gesture of defeat when she noticed them waiting in the lobby. She trudged with fatigue toward the desk.

"May I help you folks?" she asked as she puzzled over their identity.

"Yes," replied Arthur. "We need two rooms."

"I'm sorry but I only have one vacant room. Do you want it?"

"Miss O'Brian will take it."

"But Arthur, where will you stay?"

"Don't worry. I'll find a place."

"No! You can't sleep just anyplace. I ... "

"Folks, I can't stand here all night while you argue," said the woman. "I got customers running out my ears. The girl that worked for me up and left and I've had to be both cook and waitress 'til I can find someone to replace her."

"Do you have a position open?" asked Rebecca eagerly. "I need a job and I could start right now."

"Well, I don't know." Eyeing the soft hands and neat appearance, she realized Rebecca was a lady. "It's hard work and long hours."

"I can do it. Please, I need the job."

"Now, Miss Becky," interrupted Arthur, "you don't ... "

"Arthur, he's not going to show up and I have to work."

"If you want the job, it includes a room and your meals," said Molly. "Here's the key to your room, Sir." She handed a key to Arthur. "Come on, girl. We got work to do." She headed toward the kitchen with Rebecca running to keep up. "Here, put this on." She handed her an over-sized apron. "Take this pot of coffee and refill everyone's cup. Then clear off the dirty tables."

The rest of the evening was a frenzied rush. Rebecca was exhausted from the train trip, then the distressful wait at the station. She struggled to stay on her feet until closing time. Near midnight the dining room was cleaned and swept, clean table-cloths placed on the tables, and the dishes washed and put away.

Molly Bailey showed Rebecca to her room, handing her some clean sheets. "Get some rest, Girl. Breakfast comes early."

The exhausted Rebecca managed to change the sheets, then, fully clothed, she collapsed on the narrow cot. Sleep instantly overcame her weary body.

◆◆

It seemed only minutes before Molly came bustling into the room carrying a pitcher of fresh water. "I don't even know your name, Girl," she said as she set the pitcher on the rickety washstand. She smiled at the sleepy-eyed Rebecca in her wrinkled gray suit.

"Rebecca O'Brian." She stood wearily and poured some water in the bowl.

"You look like a Rebecca. Where you from? Is that your father that was with you?"

"I came from West Virginia. Arthur is an old friend from back home who escorted me out here to Colorado. He's become as close as a father to me."

"Well, I'm sure glad you showed up last night. I was just 'bout at the end of my rope."

"I appreciate you giving me the job, Mrs. Bailey."

"Call me Molly. I just don't understand why a pretty girl like you needs a job. You should be married and have a bunch of kids hanging to your skirt-tail."

"It's a long story, Molly," Rebecca said evasively.

"Well, you sure came in handy last night. Today you take the orders, deliver the food, and keep the coffee cups filled. By next week you should be broke in real good. We'll really be busy the Fourth of July 'cause of the big shindig."

Molly rushed toward the kitchen, leaving Rebecca to freshen up. She put on a brown calico dress and then pulled her hair back in a neat bun. Sitting on the edge of the cot she pulled on her high-top boots. She wished for more comfortable shoes to work in. *I'll see if Arthur can bring my trunk from the station.*

They were steadily busy all day, and late that evening while cleaning the dining area, a couple of cowhands walked in. A short, stocky man with graying red hair accompanied a tall, lean man of Swedish descent. The pale blue eyes of the blond-headed man followed Rebecca around the room. She hurried to clear the tables and escape his gaze by slipping into the kitchen.

"Those fellows are two regulars," said Molly, "and I already have their plates ready. You keep your eyes open 'round that good-lookin' Charlie, though. He likes his women," she cautioned Rebecca.

"Thanks for the warning, Molly." She headed toward their table with two heaping plates.

"Well, well, what do we have here!" said Charlie

with admiration as he watched Rebecca approach. "I wonder where Molly found this sweetheart?" He gave his companion a sly wink.

She served their food, giving Charlie a wary smile. She'd started toward the kitchen when Charlie grabbed her hand and pulled her down on his lap. "Don't be in such a hurry, Lady. I want to get to know ya a little better."

She struggled to escape, anger flashing in her green eyes. Molly rushed from the kitchen shouting, "Charlie Cooper, get your hands off Rebecca this minute." She lumbered toward them. "I didn't hire this little gal for you to manhandle."

"Rebecca?" Charlie questioned, glancing with surprise toward Dave.

"Yes, Rebecca O'Brian." Molly watched the angry Rebecca rush to the kitchen. "She just came in from back east and I don't want you fellows scaring her off. That Prissy up and ran off with some drifter, and I was real lucky that Rebecca happened in and needed work."

"Don't worry, Molly." Dave gave Charlie a warning look. "I'll see that he's on his best behavior."

Molly, reassured that everything was under control, slipped off her apron and went out the front door.

"Charlie, do you know who she is! That's the boss's bride ..."

"There comes our coffee," said Charlie loudly, drowning out Dave's comment as he saw her coming with the coffeepot. "Ma'am, I want to apologize for my rudeness. I sure don't want to get started off on the wrong foot with such a pretty lady. Will ya forgive me?"

She glanced his way, surprised to read sincerity in his eyes. "I hope it won't happen again. I'm not used to being treated with such disrespect." She busied herself around the room, keeping their cups filled and later brought out some pie Molly had set aside for them.

"Charlie, we gotta get that Josh in here and show him what he's turnin' down," whispered Dave as he fidgeted in his seat. "She's the prettiest little lady that's hit this town in a long time."

"Yeah," said Charlie with a thoughtful expression, "But Josh don't relish folks nosin' in his business, especially when it comes to women. I think what he needs is a good dose of jealousy." A devious chuckle escaped. "If we can get him in here, then I'll start acting real chummy with her. If he's any man at all he'll protect her honor."

<hr/>

The days passed and Rebecca soon fell into a routine. Arthur took a job at the hotel as a clerk—his distinguished appearance was an asset—but he continued to board at Molly's. Rebecca's good looks brought in new customers, many local cowhands, but her standoffish attitude kept them at bay while she went about her duties.

Chapter Seven

Tired and dusty, Josh looked down on the town of Longmont at dusk. Three days had passed since he had awakened to a blanket of stars overhead. His mount stood faithfully by his side, head hung low. The tumble down the mountainside had left him unconscious for several hours and his mount with a maimed foreleg. He had managed to maneuver himself and his horse to a small stream in a grassy glen. There he doctored Duchess's swollen leg, applying a compress. With a throbbing head, his bruised body aching, he had stretched out on his bedroll and had soon fallen asleep. Two days passed before they had recovered enough to get around.

Josh realized he had felt the chastening hand of God. He knew he had been reproved for his cowardly actions concerning Rebecca and also for his neglect of God. With a burdened heart he vowed that in the future he would endeavor to serve him faithfully, to set aside a time to read the Scripture and pray for guidance. He knew it would only bring peace to his soul and blessings from God.

He'd heard there was a new young preacher, Jonathan Smith, who had started a church in the lower valley. Everyone was talking about the new church, and he felt drawn to attend and discover what was drawing such great crowds. With his life turned over to God, and a new peace in his heart, he had headed down into the valley toward town.

He walked into Molly's, taking a seat near the window. He rested his weary head in his hands. He didn't notice the young woman approach his table, but as she poured him a glass of cold water, then a steaming cup of coffee he thought, *What pretty hands* as he observed the long slender fingers tipped with shell pink nails. *They haven't seen much hard work. Molly must have someone new helping her.* He glanced up to see who was waiting on him. His penetrating blue eyes locked briefly with the bewitching green eyes. With a slight blush, she rushed off to the kitchen.

He gazed out the window. People were already getting the town prepared for the big Fourth of July celebration. *I guess the men and I will come in for the celebration.* Looking back over the dining area, he admired the young woman as she served a couple of men across the room. She wearily ran the back of her hand across her forehead and then tucked back a stray wisp of red-gold hair. She was taller than the average woman with a slender body and tiny waist, but well endowed with womanly features, giving her a sensuous appearance. A sprinkling of freckles stood out on her pale, tired face as she came toward him. She gave him a slight smile as she refilled his cup. He felt a tingling sensation pass through his body. As she walked away he thought, *If Matt had sent someone like that, I might have been tempted.* He chuckled to himself.

He felt Molly's heavy tread before he saw her ambling over to his table.

"Boy, where you been keeping yourself?" she asked. She pulled out a chair across from him and sat down wearily. "I made your favorite chicken pie this weekend and you didn't even show up."

"Well, I headed up to Ghost Canyon to try gettin' a couple mares out of that wild herd but ended up lying at the bottom of a ravine. Duchess lost her footing and we sure took a tumble. I had to lie 'round couple days 'til we recovered. Is that a good 'nough excuse, Molly?"

"Serves you right for going off like that by yourself," she said gruffly, but she couldn't hide the concern in her eyes. She had taken Josh under her wing, so to speak, when he had arrived in Longmont six years ago. "Hey, Girl," she shouted to Rebecca across the room, "bring my boy a big plate of supper." Molly leaned across the table toward Josh, "Ain't she a pretty little thing," she whispered with a twinkle in her eye. "Ain't married either."

"Now, Molly, don't you start your matchmaking," said Josh with a laugh. He watched the woman approach with a heaping plate of food and set it down in front of him.

"Girl, this is one of my boys," Molly said with a laugh, giving Josh's hand a pat. "And this is Rebecca O'Brian. She just came in from the East. Can't figure why she picked this town, but I'm sure glad she did. That worthless Prissy took off last week leaving me with no help. You okay, Son?" she asked, noticing his pained expression.

"Yeah," he answered as he watched Rebecca walk over to the other table. "I'm just hungry. Gotta get some food down me and then head out to the ranch."

"Well, eat up, Boy, and I'll see if I can't scrounge up a piece of apple pie."

What a fool I've been. He watched Rebecca gracefully hurry about the room clearing away the dirty dishes. *I should've known Matt had good taste in women. I'll just tell her I had to be away from the ranch and couldn't meet her.*

Charlie and a couple of the men came in as Josh was mulling this over. Charlie hurried over to his table. "Where you been, Boss? We were startin' to worry a grizzly had got ya." He nosily pulled out a chair and flopped down, pitching his dusty hat on a nearby table. "Hey, Rebecca, bring your hungry man some food," he shouted across the room. Leaning across the table toward Josh he said in a lustful tone, "I'd sure like that little gal to warm my bed this winter."

"Shut up, Charlie." Josh said angrily. "Can't you tell she's a lady?" *How'd Charlie get acquainted with her so quick?* Josh thought. He watched her approach with three heaping plates and a coffeepot balanced precariously in her arms.

"Thank you, Little Woman," said Charlie, affectionately patting her behind. Rebecca jumped back and glared angrily at Charlie. Before she could say anything, Josh jumped up, knocking over his chair as he grabbed the front of Charlie's shirt. "Keep your dirty hands off the lady if you want to keep workin' for me," he said through clenched teeth. Righting his chair, he ignored the quickly exchanged glances as he resumed eating. Rebecca smiled her appreciation.

"Well, Joshua Holt," replied Charlie with an exaggerated sneer, "You'd think the lady belonged to you."

Josh nervously glanced at Rebecca and saw the anger flash in her eyes as she realized who he was. She slammed the coffeepot on the table, splashing scalding coffee down the front of his shirt, then fled the room.

"Now see what you've done, you oaf. What are you men doing in town anyway?" Grabbing Charlie by the arm he pushed him toward the door. Charlie, assuming an angry stance, turned and punched him on the nose, sending him sprawling across the room knocking over tables and chairs. Molly rushed from the kitchen at the commotion with Rebecca close behind.

"What's going on here!" shouted Molly. Rebecca eyed Josh's prone figure and bloody nose with disgust and then returned to the kitchen.

"Sorry, Molly," said Charlie with a guilty look. "Boss here started it, so he'll have to settle with you." He rushed out the door while the other cowhands resumed eating with sheepish grins.

"Josh, you know I don't allow no fightin' in 'ere. Just look at this place! And I wanted you to make a good impression on Rebecca." Molly fussed and fumed as he straightened the tables and chairs, then solemnly walked out.

⚫

Rebecca banged the pots and pans as she raged over her humiliation. *That pompous, arrogant bloke! What makes him think he can just march in here pretending his innocence! If he didn't want to marry me at least he could have told me to my face.* The tears begin to fall as she doused the dirty dishes in the hot sudsy water. *Lord, why'd you send me out here to be humiliated? I trusted you and look what happened,* she thought bitterly as her fleshly nature emerged.

The back door opened and Arthur quietly walked in. His heart went out to her as he registered her tears and look of despair.

"Miss Becky, this work is too hard on you. We can easily get by on what I make at the hotel until something more appropriate becomes available. You tell Molly that you quit."

"Why, Arthur, I couldn't do that to Molly. She gave me this job without knowing anything about me and I wouldn't think of leaving her with no one to help. And I won't let you support me, either. Besides, I don't mind the work. It keeps my mind from drifting to unpleasant things...like Joshua Holt! He came in for supper tonight and let me wait on him like nothing had happened. Can you believe the nerve of that man?"

"He was in here tonight?" Arthur asked as he watched Rebecca take her anger out on the tub of dirty dishes.

"Yes, and the last I saw of him, he was sprawled on the floor nursing a bloody nose. One of his own men punched him, laying him flat on his backside." She paused, leaning wearily on the wooden tub. "Arthur, I thought this was what the Lord wanted me to do, but if it was, he sure pulled a dirty trick on me."

"Now Miss Becky, don't be disrespectful," scolded Arthur with a frown. *It's not like her to doubt God! Lord,* he silently prayed, *draw her back to you and give her assurance of your divine love.* He patted her on the shoulder and smiled, "Now give me a big smile and a plate of Molly's good cooking."

"Get out of here," she said returning his smile, "or I'll let you go without supper."

He chuckled as he went into the dining area, choosing a seat near the window. Molly stood by a table where two men sat. She glanced at Arthur but continued to converse with the men. Arthur began to catch the drift of their conversation and undertook to hear all he could.

"You mean to tell me that my Rebecca came out here to marry Josh!" said Molly with astonishment.

"Yeah, but Boss didn't know anything 'bout it," said Dave shaking his head. "At least not 'till Charlie brought Matt's telegram. She was due in the next morning.

"Boss got cold feet real fast, didn't he, Dave," laughed Brad, a small, wiry man in his forties.

"Yeah, he left early the next mornin' to look for that herd of wild horses. He didn't know that Charlie had already read that wire and Josh left it right there on the table where I couldn't 'elp but read it, too."

"Sure, Dave," laughed Molly.

"Well, me and Charlie got our heads 'gether and 'cided the only way to bring him to his senses was to make him jealous. Gosh, Charlie sure hates actin' so boorish with that little gal just to make Josh jealous. He said he hoped she wouldn't 'ave hard feelin' toward 'im when she finds out the truth."

"You should've seen his face when I introduced her," said Molly, remembering Josh's reaction. "I figur'd somethin' was wrong. He mumbled somethin' 'bout bein' real hungry and gettin' back to the ranch."

"He must not be in too big of a hurry," grinned Dave. "I see him pacin' back and forth in front of ya place here, Molly."

"Don't you fellows be too rough on my boy,"

laughed Molly, causing her round belly to shake. "It looks like he's got it real bad. I wonder if the old man over there knows about Josh," she whispered. "He escort'd her out here from back east."

"I wondered who that old man was," said Brad. "Dave, we'd better get out of here. I think Boss is waitin' for us to leave. Molly, you hold down the fort, and me and Dave will get on home and do some prayin'."

"You'll have to do the prayin', Brad," said Dave, sadly. "Me and him ain't been on very good speakin' terms lately."

<hr />

The dining room cleared, and Arthur warily watched the tall, well-built man pacing restlessly in front of the boarding house. *So that's how things are.* He smiled as he thought about what he had overheard. Rebecca came with his supper and a cup of coffee. He smiled again as he watched her look out the window to where Josh stood with a dejected look. He observed the flash of anger in her eyes, but it was quickly followed by a look of interest—a hint of yearning. She fled toward the refuge of the kitchen as Josh started toward Molly's porch.

When he had left Molly's earlier, Josh had determined to go home, climb into bed, and forget the woman ever existed. He was exhausted, dusty, and downhearted. He gingerly felt his nose, vowing vengeance on the unsuspecting Charlie. Everything had gone smoothly over the past few years and now, all it had taken was a pretty woman to completely mess up his life and his mind. *I can't go home and leave her with a bad impression. I wish Brad and Dave would leave, then…* Glancing in the window he saw them getting up to leave. He slipped into the shadow of the building and watched them ride out of town. He felt self-conscious and foolish as he entered the room. He sighed with relief when he realized only an elderly man occupied it. He felt the eyes of the man boring into his soul, and he shifted uneasily and then headed toward a table in back.

"Come give a lonely old man some company, Son."

Josh hesitated, then slowly walked over and pulled out a chair.

"Arthur Byron," he introduced himself, reaching out his hand.

"Joshua Holt," responded Josh, taking the pale, blue-veined hand in his.

"Yes, I've heard of you, Son," smiled Arthur.

"Aren't you a stranger in town?" he asked with a puzzled look.

"Yes, I arrived last week. I'm really impressed with your beautiful country. The mountains…such majestic mountains. You probably don't realize how blessed you are to live in this rugged country. I left a position in the city and came out west just to end up as a desk clerk. Still stuck inside from daylight 'til dark," he sighed.

"Well, Mr. Byron, I doubt you could find a job

better suited for a man your age," smiled Josh, beginning to enjoy the man's company.

"What do you know about age? I could work you down any day, young man," he said with a sheepish grin. "I want to work outside. Maybe be a cowboy." Realizing Josh was trying to keep from laughing at him, he added, "But raising a garden and flowers are my passion. I'm also an apiarist."

"A what?" Josh was not acquainted with the occupation.

"An apiarist. Beekeeper," he replied, laughing at Josh's puzzled expression.

"Oh, you had me there for a moment. A beekeeper, huh?" He looked at him keenly. "I have a place out of town a ways. Right now I have twelve stands of bees scattered throughout my orchard. I'd give you a job, but I'm not able to take on another hand right now."

Molly came out with a fresh pot of coffee and a slice of pie, setting it down for Arthur. She placed her work-roughened hands on her ample hips and glared at Josh. "I want to have a word with you, Boy."

"What have I done now, Molly?" he asked. He poured himself a cup of coffee and missed the warning glance Arthur gave her.

"Well, we'll talk about it later, but you'd best be prepared for an earful," she said before heading back toward the kitchen.

Josh looked at Arthur with an impish grin. "Molly treats me like the son she never had. When I arrived in Longmont she just assumed the role of stand-in mother and she doesn't let me get by with much."

"Don't you have a wife and family?" He poured another cup of coffee.

"No," he replied, absentmindedly swirling the grounds in the bottom of his cup. He thought of Rebecca and said hesitantly, "I could have married a beautiful woman, but my cowardly actions ruined my chances. My brother Matt found me a bride back east and, when she arrived, I was too scared to show up."

"You mean you couldn't find a wife for yourself?" He watched the changing expressions on the young man's face.

"But I didn't want a wife! At least, not until I saw what I had turned down," he added sadly. "She is so beautiful. And she's a real lady. Although, I did discover she has a real temper," he chuckled.

"What you need to do, young man, is walk right in there and tell the lady how you feel and ask her to forgive you."

Josh looked at Arthur with a startled expression. "How'd you know who I was talkin' about?"

"Because I'm the one who escorted your bride out here. I've been her friend the past few years and I don't want to see her hurt. She came out here in faith that this was where God wanted her. Now she doubts God, questions his guidance, and her faith is weakening. That is not like my Miss Becky. If you admire her as much as you say, then you need to get things smoothed out. I think she knows you are out here, so, when Molly comes out, you just march in there and face that little spitfire," he chuckled.

Josh sat in deep thought. He didn't notice when Arthur left the table and headed up to his room. Taking a deep breath as Molly came out, he walked over to her and slipped his arm around her plump shoulders. "Be a good little mamma and stay out of the kitchen for a while. That is, unless you hear me hollering for help." Giving the curious Molly a sheepish grin, he headed toward the back.

Chapter Eight

> *Therefore shall a man leave his father and his mother, and shall cleave unto his wife: and they shall be one flesh.*
>
> Genesis 2:24

The door from the dining room opened and assuming it was Molly, Rebecca said, "Has that dear Mr. Holt left yet? I've almost finished the dishes and I can start on the dining room as soon as he leaves." There was no reply. She turned and gasped as she saw Josh leaning against the doorjamb with a quizzical expression on his face. Color crept into her cheeks.

"Do you really hate me that much, Rebecca?" His blue eyes seemed to pierce her soul, to discover her real feelings.

"I don't hate you, Mr. Holt," she said with a toss of her head.

"I'm sorry if I've hurt you. It was never my intention to cause you any pain."

"Hurt me? You humiliated me in front of my dear friend. I assured Arthur you were a fine, honorable gentlemen. A Christian! But you didn't even care enough to meet my train. You thought you had to sneak in here and see what you were getting before you committed yourself."

"That's not true, Rebecca," Josh said with a pained expression. "I didn't even know you worked here. I didn't even know anything about you coming 'til the afternoon before you were to arrive."

"But your brother sent you a wire over a week before I left," she exclaimed.

"Maybe so, but our wire service isn't the greatest here in town. It may be days before someone is in town and picks up the wire. I received Matt's wire and yours at the same time."

"But why didn't you show up?" Tears threatened to overflow, and she turned back to the tub of dishes to hide their escape. She jumped as she felt a pair of warm, strong hands gently touch her shoulders.

"I ran scared," he sighed. "I took the coward's way out and ran to the hills. My horse slipped and fell into a deep ravine. It laid us both up for three days. I just got back today."

Rebecca turned with concern in her eyes. "Were … were you hurt?"

With a deep breath, Josh gently took her hands in his. "I just got a bump on my head, but Duchess had an injured leg. I'm not tryin' to play on your feelings or make excuses. I just want you to know how ashamed I am for my actions. I acted like Jonah. Running away from God and what he had planned for my life. But he stopped me in my flight and kept me in one place until I repented. I've vowed to put him first in my life from now on. I pray that you can forgive me and give me another chance. I want you to be my wife."

"Mr. Holt, I ... I'm ... "

"Josh. Call me Josh," he smiled.

"Josh," she said timidly. "We need to talk."

"I thought we were," he grinned.

"Don't laugh at me. You make me nervous." She tried to keep a sober face.

"Let's step out on the back porch where it's cooler," he suggested with a glance at the door that led to the dining room, then said a little louder, "That way Molly can't have her ear pressed to the door, eavesdropping." They both grinned as they heard Molly's heavy tread scurry away.

They stepped out on the porch, and he moved a woven basket off an old rocker so she could sit down. He took a seat on the step at her feet and then leaned cautiously against the rickety porch post.

"Josh," she started, "I want you to know why I didn't wait until next spring and travel out with your brother and his family." She took a deep breath. "My uncle recently died, and his stipulation for me to inherit his home was that I marry his business partner, George Pickett. George is a cruel, wicked man who succeeded in keeping his true nature hidden from Uncle Hess. But his evil ways have been revealed to me many times as he has tried to persuade me to marry him. I've always refused his offers. I'm convinced he's the one who persuaded Uncle Hess to put that in his will. He went away on business and told me to be ready for the wedding when he got back. I don't love him and I won't marry him! I had to get away without him being able to trace me. He is a persistent and determined man when it comes to getting his way. Then I met your brother, and here I am."

"But," said Josh with a thoughtful expression, "You said you wouldn't marry him because you didn't love him. You don't love me, so why are you willing to marry me?"

"I believe I can learn to love you," replied Rebecca as she gazed into his deep blue eyes. "Matthew told me you were a good Christian man. I gave this decision much thought and prayer, and this is the way God has led me. I couldn't believe this was his will, for me to come out west and marry a stranger, but everything just fell into place as if it were meant to be."

"I was pretty angry when I got Matt's wire. I was sure you would be an ugly old school marm," he grinned.

"Well you're right about that part. I am a schoolteacher, and—"

"But," he interrupted with admiration in his eyes, "you're beautiful!" He looked away, embarrassed at his bold words. He gazed up toward the moonlit hills as a coyote's call wailed, then turned back to her. "I turned it all over to God, and suddenly, I wasn't angry anymore. If this marriage is God's will, then we'd best do his will. Rebecca, I'll be a good husband to you, if you will marry me."

"I want you to be sure." She felt the tears threaten to escape. "I believe that marriage is a lifelong commitment and one to be honored."

"So do I, Rebecca." He looked into her green eyes filled with tears. "And it will be honored on my part. Will you marry me this Friday?"

"Friday?" she asked with a tremor in her voice. "That's just two days away!"

"You can be ready." He stood and took her hand. "Let's go tell Molly before she dies of curiosity."

As they walked into the dining room, Arthur and Molly stood by the window, quietly conferring. They looked toward the couple with guilty expressions as they walked in.

"Now, I wonder what they're talkin' so seriously about?" Josh grinned as Molly busied herself with straightening a tablecloth. Arthur picked up a cold cup of coffee, took a sip, and then shuddered at the taste. "Do you think we should tell them about the wedding, or just slip off and find a preacher?" he asked Rebecca mischievously.

"Wedding?" Molly silently mouthed the words. "Yieeeek," she squealed. She rushed toward them, then threw her arms around their necks. "I can't believe it!" She cast a frown toward Josh and said, "You're not pulling my leg again are you, Josh?"

"All I have to do is ask Mr. Byron for his permission, and then, find a preacher for Friday." He looked at Arthur, who curiously watched Rebecca.

"Can you find some new help and have this gal ready for the wedding in two days, Molly?"

"I sure can, Mr. Byron," Molly said. "That sister of Prissy's been in twice asking for a job."

Josh looked tenderly at Rebecca. "I gotta get home. We'll all be back in town tomorrow afternoon for the big Fourth celebration, so I'll see you then." He walked with a lighthearted step out the front door.

The excited Molly headed back to the kitchen, and Arthur asked with concern, "Is everything going to be all right, Miss Becky?"

"Yes, Arthur," she answered with a slight smile. "I believe he is a good man."

———◆———

The town was filling up for the celebration of the country's independence, and soon Molly's dining room bustled with business. Molly had hired Prudy, and she was busy in the kitchen.

Rebecca sat talking with Arthur over a late lunch when the young preacher Jonathan Smith walked into Molly's.

"Well, good morning, friends," he called, with a surprised smile. "I didn't expect to run into you folks again, but it's a nice surprise."

"It's a pleasure to see you again, Brother Smith." Arthur stood and shook the preacher's hand as Rebecca looked on with a smile. "Is this where your church is located?"

"About seven miles out of town. Shadow Valley Baptist Church. Are you staying here in Longmont?"

"Yes," Arthur said as he cast a questioning glance at Rebecca. "Miss Becky here is going to be married to a rancher who lives near here."

"Congratulations!" Jonathan said and took her hand in his. "I wish you much happiness."

Rebecca saw Josh as he walked into the dining room and quickly pulled her hand away. She looked at Josh and smiled.

"Brother Smith, this is Joshua Holt, who has asked me to marry him. Josh, Brother Smith is a preacher we met in Denver."

"Jonathan Smith?" Josh questioned. "I've heard a lot about you and your church. I've thought about coming down to your church."

"That's great," replied Smith. "There's no better way to start a marriage than to be in the Lord's house on Sunday."

"Well," Josh looked anxiously at Rebecca, "the preacher here in town is gone for a week to his brother's funeral, so we may not be able to get married until he gets back."

"Why, I'll marry you," Smith offered. "That is, if you want me to."

Josh looked at Rebecca. "I'd like that," she said as she turned to Smith. "I feel like I've already known you a long time, and I would feel more comfortable with you than with a complete stranger."

"Great! When do I get the honor?"

"Would tomorrow morning be all right?" asked Josh.

"It sure would. I planned on staying in town with some friends tonight, anyway."

They discussed plans for a few minutes, and then Rebecca went to the kitchen to help with supper, leaving the men to become better acquainted.

Molly's place bustled all evening, and it was close to ten before Molly and Rebecca could lock the door and slip down the street to where they heard music playing. As they stood on the edge of the crowd, Rebecca caught sight of Josh just as a small, dark-haired woman walked up to him and slipped her arm possessively through his. Rebecca's anger began to rise, until she noticed Josh push the woman firmly away. The woman lashed out at him angrily before she pushed her way through the crowd and disappeared.

Several minutes passed before Josh spied Rebecca in the crowd and slipped over to her side. She felt a wave of pride as she noticed several of the young women glance their way enviously.

Dave and Charlie stood several feet away. They grinned and slapped each other on the back as they saw the look that passed between Josh and Rebecca.

"Looks like you might jist get out of cookin' for us hogs after all," said Charlie with a laugh. Dave danced a little jig, then grabbed the nearest woman and danced her around until she was breathless. Her husband finally rescued her, but Dave quickly found another victim.

The celebration ended later that night with a fireworks display, and then everyone headed for home.

———◆———

Josh watched in wonder as Rebecca descended the stairs on Arthur's arm. She was dressed in a cream-colored wedding dress and carried a simple bouquet of flowers. The slightly yellowed dress had belonged to Rebecca's mother, and Molly had picked the flowers from her garden out back.

Rebecca paused in the doorway of Molly's parlor with a look of panic.

Josh saw the fear in her eyes. But the fear faded when she looked at him and smiled. She walked across the room and stood by his side.

A short while later, they emerged from Molly's parlor as husband and wife. Josh looked across the street and caught Charlie's attention, beckoning him over.

"Charlie, Rebecca and I were just married." Charlie grinned and winked at Rebecca. Josh frowned at him and continued. "Get Rebecca's trunk from the house, then go to the station and pick up the other trunks that are stored there. And get Arthur's too." He turned to Arthur and said, "You might as well stay with us until you decide what you really want to do."

Rebecca blinked away the tears of gratitude as she watched an excited Arthur climb onto the wagon seat with Charlie. The next few days would be a lot easier just to know that he would be near.

The man from the livery drove a buggy in front

of Molly's with Duchess tied to the back. Josh helped Rebecca into the buggy and tucked her skirt away from the wheel. Then he climbed in beside her, took the reins, and started out of town as friends shouted congratulations and waved.

They reached a quiet country road; Rebecca looked about curiously. "How far is it to your ranch?"

"It's about a two hour ride to *our* ranch," he answered. "I hope you'll be happy there, Rebecca. It's not a fancy house, and I plan to make improvements, as I'm able. I purchased the property from a widow, Sarah Daniels, five years ago. She wanted to go back East after her husband died. She left everything in the house and took her seven children and went back to Boston to live with her brother. I'm afraid I've neglected the house, and I didn't have time to hire anybody to clean it before you got here."

"Well, I'm glad you didn't," interrupted Rebecca. "A wife wouldn't be much benefit if you had to hire someone to get the work done. Just supply me with plenty of water and I'll take care of it."

With a chuckle, he responded, "I'll see that Dave keeps in plenty of water. You'll need it!"

In the shimmering noonday heat, they topped a ridge and stopped to look down over a valley where a field of golden wheat waved a greeting. On a knoll were buildings and barns and a two-story log house. A porch extended across the front and around one side.

"This is home," was all he said. He picked up the reins and urged the horse and buggy down the hill.

Chapter Nine

> *She looketh well to the ways of her household, and eateth not the bread of idleness.*
>
> Proverbs 31:27

As they pulled up to the front of the house, Dave rushed from the barn. He cast a glance of admiration toward Rebecca, then turned to Josh. "Boss," he said, his breath coming in short gasps, "you'd better come. Nugget's not doing too well." He shuffled uneasily on his feet. "Did you see Charlie in town?"

"Yes, he's bringing the trunks and a visitor." Josh saw the wagon top the hill. "There he is now. Dave, you get some help to unload the wagon and send Charlie right over to the barn." He turned to Rebecca. "Sorry, but this is a good mare, and I don't want to lose her. Just go on in and I'll be along as soon as I can."

Rebecca opened the front door and entered a large room that she quickly deemed the center of activity in the house. At one end of the room was a huge, stone fireplace with a rough-hewn mantel. The opening was large enough to step into. Over the mantel a gun rested on a rack of antlers. The mantel held a jumble of items. Inside the opening of the fireplace, a pot of savory stew simmered, and from a Dutch oven near the hot coals the aroma of baked cornbread escaped. From the mantel hung pots and skillets with legs. It was evident that this was where most of the meals were prepared.

On each side of the fireplace were large cupboards with open shelves above and doors below. On the shelves were a variety of dishes, jugs, stoneware, and mugs, along with wooden utensils. Under the window at the front of the house was a sideboard with an oil lamp and a white enamel basin of water. Out from the fireplace sat a long sawbuck table with a thick, plank-like top made of oak. The finish, if there ever had been one, was completely worn off, and it was embedded with grease stains and in dire need of a good scrub. Around the table was an odd collection of slat-back, split-bottom, and ladder-back chairs.

Off from this living area a potbellied stove dominated a smaller room. It held a large blue granite coffeepot, steaming and ready for anyone in need of a cup. A low table sat under a window that looked out over an orchard. It held a bucket of drinking water with a dipper. It also held two large dishpans. Judging by the pile of crusted, dirty dishes, it appeared they hadn't been used for days. A narrow door led to a porch on the back of the house.

She returned to the large living area occupied

by a wooden settee, a couple of rockers, and several split-bottom chairs. At the far end of the room she discovered a smaller fireplace with a stairway on one side that led to the upstairs, and on the other side a door leading to a large bedroom at the west end of the house. She glanced through another doorway in the back of the main room and discovered it led to a small bedroom with only an iron bed and a large wardrobe. The room looked very much lived in. Some pegs on the wall held an assortment of overalls, shirts, and coats.

The inside walls of the house were of plaster and in much need of a fresh coat of whitewash. The floor was made of wide pine boards, the color obscured by a layer of dust. Even in its disarray, the result was a warm, homey feeling from a completely male predominance.

She studied the cooking arrangement. Dave entered the front door with an eager grin on his whiskered face.

"Dave," she said, "you will have to teach me how you bake your bread without an oven. I'm sure I'll have some scorched bread the first few times."

"Not to worry, Missus," he replied with a chuckle. "I'm sure you will do just fine." *I must tell Josh that he should get his bride one of those new cast-iron cook stoves, with an oven and all. I bet she could make the best lip-smacking apple pies you ever tasted in that big oven.*

Two workhands passed through the room with bashful glances of admiration at the new missus as they carried her trunks to the large room at the end of the house. As they returned, Dave stopped and gave his stew a quick stir. The door closed behind them and Rebecca glanced out the window and saw Arthur amble toward the barn with one of the hands. He seemed to have made himself at home.

Dave seemed to have supper under control, so she entered the room where her trunks had been deposited. She was pleasantly surprised by the furnishings. Though they told a dusty tale from long disuse, their beauty could not be hidden. The furniture seemed out of place with the rest of the house. A mahogany tester bed dominated the room, and at the foot was a low blanket chest. There was also a three-drawer serpentine front dresser, with an attached beveled mirror that pivoted, and a matching chest of drawers. A small table beside the bed held a beautiful cut-glass oil lamp. A small fireplace extended from the back of the one in the front room. On one side of the fireplace was a built-in bookcase, and on the other side a clothes closet, which was under the stairway.

The room had four huge windows and a door that led to the wraparound porch, where a neat stack of firewood was kept dry under the porch roof, ready for winter. There were no curtains on the bedroom windows, or anywhere else in the house for that matter, so she quickly opened her trunk and took out a quilt. She made a place to change clothes in the corner of the room by her closet. She took off her bonnet and suit and laid them on one of her trunks, then changed into a blue cotton print dress.

She tied a work apron around her small waist and went to work with cloth smothered in furniture oil she had brought along. Quickly the dust disappeared from the beautiful furniture. The feather mattress, she carried out to the porch to air in the rays of the hot afternoon sun. A search in the kitchen area produced a straw broom, and she proceeded to sweep the floor. A cloth wrapped around the broom quickly dispensed of the cobwebs and their makers from all the corners and windows. She gave the furniture a final dust before the feather tick was brought inside, then pulled linens and a couple of quilts from her trunk and made up the bed.

She began to feel more settled, so she returned to the huge fireplace and checked the stew. Dave had been in, and the pone of cornbread sat in its pan on the hearth, covered with a cloth. She heated some water on the stove and, finding some lye soap and a scrub brush, she attacked the tabletop with vigor and prayed it would dry before suppertime. The stack of dirty dishes soon disappeared. She smiled as Dave stuck his head in the door, observed what had been done, then quickly disappeared. The kitchen worktable was scrubbed and then the water pail. She refilled the bucket with fresh water from the well beside the back porch. She discovered a wooden bowl of red-cheeked apples on a shelf and quickly peeled them and put them on to cook with plans to make fried apple pies.

Later she noticed the men lounged around the front porch, and soon Dave eased through the door and looked around the clean cook area with amazement on his face.

"Supper be ready soon, ma'am?" he asked as he sniffed the air, fragrant with the smell of apples and spices.

"Is Josh ready?"

"No, Ma'am," he replied, "he's still out with Nugget, but the boys are real hungry, especially with the smell of apple pie drifting outside."

"Oh, do I cook for all the men, too?" she asked, surprised.

"We all just eat here together," Dave answered, "but I'll help this evening so you can get used to it."

"I'm sorry, I didn't know. Tell them it will be ready real soon." She hurried to set the table and put some more pies on to fry. No wonder there was such a large kettle of stew prepared.

Soon Dave, Brad, and Brent crowded around the table. They reached every which way for the food; but when they looked up at the astonished Rebecca, they paused and looked as guilty as little boys caught with their hands in the cookie jar.

Her expression quickly turned to one of amusement as she viewed the embarrassed faces.

"Shall we ask the blessing on the food first?" she asked. The men squirmed.

After a moment of silence, Dave said, "Brad there be the praying one." He pointed toward a small, wiry man in his late forties.

Brad quietly bowed his head and whispered,

"Thank you, Lord for this food and the new missus that fixed it. Amen."

The meal continued, and the men cast curious looks her way. Dave admired the clean tabletop with awe. The pies disappeared, some of them eaten before the stew. She slyly hid a few in the kitchen for Josh, Arthur, and Charlie to eat later.

"I'll take some supper out to the boss and the others," Dave said. "Too bad they had to miss out on those apple pies."

"Come back and I'll have a pot of coffee ready to take to them," Rebecca said from the kitchen as she quickly wrapped the hidden pies in a clean cloth, ready to send out with the coffee.

By the time Dave got back, she had the dishes washed and was scrubbing the cupboards by the fireplace. The dishes that had been on the shelves had disappeared to the kitchen. She planned to put the pretty dishes Mary had packed for her in their place. Dave took the pot of coffee from the stove and chuckled at her cunning when she slipped the pies in his hand.

When Dave got back to the barn, Nugget had finally given birth. A fine colt stood by her side on long, wobbly legs as he nursed with greed. The three men washed from a bucket. They gobbled the stew, then savored the delicious pies and drank the hot steaming coffee.

Josh was pleased with the knowledge and gentleness Arthur had displayed while they worked with the mare. As they toiled together, Josh gained a great deal of respect for the old gentleman and asked him to stay on at the ranch. He knew he would profit from the vast knowledge Arthur had gained over the years. He had told Arthur if he didn't want to stay in the bunkhouse with the men, he could fix up the little cabin at the back of the yard where the Danielses had lived when they first homesteaded. Arthur had looked toward the small cabin with a yearning in his eyes. He had not possessed a home of his own since he had left England at the age of nineteen. And he would be close by his Miss Becky to see that she was treated well.

When the last crumbs were eaten, Dave gathered up the dishes and coffeepot. He turned to Josh: "I bet that little wife of yours could cook up a storm if she had one of those new cook stoves like I saw at Sanford's Hardware the other day."

Josh glanced at Arthur and asked, "Is that what she's always cooked on?"

"Well, yes," he replied, "but Miss Becky can cook on anything and make it taste good. She can make the best fried chicken you've ever tasted and bake buttermilk biscuits that stand sky high."

"Then you best go into town first thing in the morning," he said to Dave, "and get her anything she needs. Tell Mr. Sanford I'll settle up with him next trip to town." Josh was surprised at his own generosity, but he figured Rebecca was well worth the expense.

Arthur volunteered to bed down in the barn to watch over the new colt for the night, so Dave and

Charlie headed for the bunkhouse. Josh stepped out of the barn and watched the sun slip down behind the house. He hurried up the stream a ways to a sparkling swimming hole, where he stepped out of his dusty clothes and dived in. The cool water refreshed his tired body. He felt revived after the long day and soon hurried toward the house. He was surprised as he stepped in and saw the difference in the room's appearance.

Rebecca reached into the bottom of a wooden barrel for the last of the dishes to put on the clean shelves. She felt his gaze and quickly stood up, but as she did, she bumped her head on the low shelf. Tears filled her eyes.

"Are you all right?" He rushed to her side and felt through her silky hair for any damage.

"I'm fine," she answered with a nervous laugh. She felt a wave of tingles rush over her body at his touch. Feeling her embarrassment, he quickly pulled his hands away.

"I'm sorry to have left you alone all afternoon, but I can see that you haven't been idle," he said as he looked around the room. She had swept the floors and dusted the furniture in the large room after supper.

He went into his room to change, and she finally got her dishes out and had placed them on the shelves when he came out dressed in a blue cotton shirt and denim jeans. When she placed the last dish on the shelf he took her by the hand and led her to a chair in front of the fire. He pulled up another in front of her and straddled it backwards.

"I have asked Arthur to stay on at the ranch," he said. "He is a wise man and, even with his being up in years, I know he will be of great value to me. He's to move into the cabin at the back of the house and seems to be real pleased."

"I'm so glad," she whispered, tears of gratitude in her eyes. "I know you won't be sorry, for he is a good man."

"Now, about us." He picked up her small trembling hand. "I want you to be completely comfortable with our marriage. If you want to wait a while until we get to know each other better before actually becoming my wife, I'll understand. Do you know what I mean?"

She looked into his blue eyes and saw his concern, but also his desire for her. She smiled and gently touched his cheek with her hand. "I'm ready to become your wife whenever you want," she said with a slight tremor in her voice. "Just the little time I've spent with you has shown me that you're really a kind and considerate man, and I appreciate that you put my feelings first."

He gently leaned forward and kissed her sweet lips. *Thank you God, for this, my beloved wife.*

With a smile he said, "It's been a long day and it's late. I'll bring in some water and lock up while you get ready for bed."

He went out the back door and Rebecca hurried to the bedroom and put on her long white nightgown in the changing corner. Josh came in and smiled as she sat on the edge of the bed brushing her hair. With all the tangles out of the red-gold strands, she braided it, and then slipped into bed. Josh smiled again as he blew out the light. Stepping out of his clothes, he climbed in between the cool, clean sheets that smelled of the fragrance of lavender they had been stored with.

He gently reached over and pulled her into his arms, her head resting on his shoulder. Soon she relaxed, and with a gentle squeeze he closed his eyes and prayed aloud. "Lord, I thank you for this day and all the blessings you have bestowed upon us. I especially want to thank you for the lovely wife you have sent my way. Lord, only you knew how much I needed her to make my life complete. Be with us and we will strive to always put you first in our lives. Amen."

Chapter Ten

> *Pride goeth before destruction, and an haughty spirit before a fall.*
>
> Proverbs 16:18

George Pickett arrived back in Morgantown. Although it was late at night he still felt the urge to ride past the two-story brick house, which now belonged to him and his soon-to-be wife. Just the thought of Rebecca put a smirk on his face as he thought of how his cunning had finally won him this coveted prize. It made him feel high and mighty to have finally put one over on her after her many refusals. He anticipated the pleasure he would feel when he removed her from her self-righteous pedestal and she was under his power and control. He had many times verbally declared his love for her, but his selfish heart could love only himself.

As he looked up at the darkened windows where he assumed everyone was asleep, pride was topmost in his mind at what he had accomplished in the last few years. Not many knew the strings he had pulled to get himself in this position, especially Hester Malone. He felt sure he could easily dominate his new wife, since she had shown no interest in her uncle's will. It had cost him quite a bit to have the lawyer stop just short of the last condition, which would have given Rebecca just the leverage she needed to escape his grasp. But she had reacted just as he had thought she would and had showed no interest to discover all that was in the will. The idea that she would still refuse him had not once entered his egotistical mind. He passed on by the darkened house without a clue that it was void of any occupants.

He woke up early the next morning and looked around the room of his shabby boarding house with disdain. He gloated over the fact that he would soon be able to leave this modest dwelling and live somewhere more suited to his position in society. He quickly dressed and went down to his last greasy breakfast in Mrs. Hall's dining room. He looked forward to the delectable meals he knew Mary could prepare, having had dined many times at Hester Malone's table.

He wore a contemptuous smile on his way to his newly possessed estate. When he arrived, he swaggered up to the front door and gave the impressive brass lion's head a knock that resounded through the empty house.

"Where is that worthless Arthur?" he mumbled to himself. He determined to have a talk with the man as soon as he took over and would see that there was no slothfulness on the part of the servants.

After a second knock, he angrily stomped around to the back entrance of the house and again got no response.

"That's just like Rebecca," he muttered to himself, "to let all the servants off on the same day. I wonder where she could be? Probably over to the Rileys' to gossip with that old, pompous windbag."

Not certain when she would be back, he decided to go to town and take care of some neglected business. He stopped at the law office first, and when he entered Jake Roberts's private office he suddenly felt he was about to hear bad news.

"Mr. Pickett," the lawyer said hesitantly as he pulled an envelope from his drawer, "I received these keys in the mail a few days after you left town. I knew you would be gone a few weeks, so I took it upon myself to go over and check on things. The house was vacant with no hint of where everyone had gone. I have inquired around town and found that the cook, Mary, has started to work for the Satterfields. I went to see her, and she said the other girl had taken a job on the other side of town to care for some children whose mother was terribly ill. She said she didn't know where Miss O'Brian or the old butler had gone, but I feel she knows more than she let on."

George cut loose with a round of profanities that made even the hardened lawyer squirm in his seat. "If she thinks she is going to get away from me this easy, she is being very foolish," he shouted as he stomped around the room, his face livid with rage.

"I've worked too long on this deal to let her mess it up now." He realized he had let out too much information in front of the crafty lawyer. He grabbed the keys and stomped out of the room.

Rebecca had few friends besides the Rileys, so he immediately started to their place, convinced he would find her there. Agnes Riley answered the door, surprised at the identity of her caller.

"I wish to speak with Miss O'Brian," he said, with a hint of superiority in his voice.

"Rebecca?" she questioned. "She's not here, and come to think of it, I haven't talked to her for several weeks. Why did you think she was here?"

"Now, come, Mrs. Riley," he answered with a smirk, "you can't fool me. I know you are aware of her exact whereabouts."

"I beg your pardon, Sir." She realized he thought she knew more than she did. "I do not like being called a liar right on my own porch. It would be best if you leave now." She firmly closed and locked the door. He stood there a second with a surprised but aggravated expression on his face.

He quickly rode back to town, determined to get to the bottom of the mystery of her disappearance at any cost.

<hr>

Back at the lawyer's office, Jake Roberts had pulled Hester Malone's will from his file and started to read it over again. The last condition on the will—the one that George had paid him not to read aloud—stated that if Rebecca and George did not marry, the house was to be sold and the proceeds divided between them. This was the last thing George had wanted because his greatest desire was to have Rebecca and the house in his possession.

Chapter Eleven

> *In all things shewing thyself a pattern of good works.*
>
> Titus 2:7a

Rebecca awoke the next morning as Josh got out of bed to get dressed. She blushed slightly as she remembered what had taken place between them the night before. As soon as Josh left the room, she jumped out of bed and ran to the changing corner where she had laid out clean underclothes, a lavender and white calico dress, and a crisp white apron. Josh greeted her with a tender smile as she came into the kitchen where he was stoking the fire. She filled the coffeepot and put it on, then turned to a bowl where she had mixed up some buckwheat mix and left it to rise overnight. She did not intend to be caught again with hungry men waiting for food. Josh gave her a light kiss on the forehead as he headed out the door. Dave had shown her where most of the supplies were kept, and she soon had sausage in a skillet in the fireplace and a stack of hotcakes quickly piled up on a platter. She had just finished a platter of fried eggs when she heard the men file into the room and sit down at the table. Josh came in a few minutes later, paused to observe the piles of food she had prepared, and with a tender look toward his bride, he said, "Men you'd best enjoy this meal because tomorrow it's back to Dave's cooking for you all."

"Now just a minute, Boss," shouted Dave. He jumped up, and his chair landed with a bang. "That wasn't in the deal!"

"And what deal was that?" Josh asked. He tried to keep the grin from his face as he watched Dave's frustrated expression. "I don't remember making any deal with you lately."

"But I always thought when you got married, I wouldn't have to cook for this bunch of hogs!"

"Well, Dave, old man, you were wrong again!" laughed Josh as Dave picked up his chair and slumped down in despair. "This little gal married me, not the whole lot of you. When you get back from town with that new fancy stove you talked me into buying, you can take that old potbellied stove out to the bunkhouse and fix up a kitchen for yourself."

With a smile of appreciation to Dave, Rebecca said, "Don't look so down-hearted. If you talked Josh into buying me a new stove, you can be sure you will eat many a meal cooked on it. You can all count on eating at our table at least twice a week for sure."

With a mixture of shouts and whistles, the men showed their approval and waited for Josh to sit down.

"Let's eat, men," he said, then noticed their questioning look toward Rebecca.

"We gotta ask the blessing first," interrupted Dave. "That is if you want to eat the missus' cookin'. She done laid the law down to us yesterday."

With a smile of appreciation to his wife, Josh bowed his head and asked the blessing. Soon the hearty breakfast had disappeared, and as the sun peeked over the hills in the east, the men headed out to work.

———◆◆———

After the dishes had been washed and put away, Rebecca made the bed and then hurried outside to explore. Outside the kitchen door was a well with a moss-covered shingled roof over its cobblestone box. A bucket connected by rope to a crank made easy work of drawing up water. Off the porch were steps that led down into a cool, musty cellar under the house. In a small smokehouse nearby were hams hung from the ceiling ready to be baked and served to a hungry crew. On the path toward the necessary house was the chicken coop where a healthy flock of Rhode Island Reds resided. Out back was a fine stand of fruit trees, and scattered throughout the orchard were stands of beehives that buzzed with activity. What little grass there had been around the house had not long survived the trample of horse and rider.

Out by the orchard was a small cabin nestled in a group of trees that resembled a child's playhouse when compared to the main house. She saw that the door and windows were open and decided to walk over to see if this was where Arthur was to live. As she drew closer she could see the dust fly out the door and knew that Arthur was hard at work. He heard her approach and came to the door with a happy grin on his dirt-smudged face. His white shirt was dirty and wrinkled. She had never caught him in such disarray before, and she laughed with glee at his appearance.

"Don't laugh, now, Miss Becky." He tried to look stern. "It won't look like this long. Just wait until I get my trunks up from the barn and unpacked. This will look just like home."

"Oh, Arthur," she said as she tried to keep her laughter under control, "I'm laughing at your disheveled appearance, not your home. I know it will look real homey when you get finished. I'm so glad you are to stay on at the ranch. That way I can be sure you don't try to overdo yourself." With a quick hug and a peck on his smudged cheek, she turned to view the interior of his new home.

There was a stone fireplace at one end of the room and a small stove at the back. A rusty, iron bed filled one corner, and a row of pegs on the wall indicated a place for hanging clothes. A huge rocker, a small table, and two split-bottom chairs completed the furnishings. On the front porch was a metal wash pan hanging on a nail next to a cracked mirror. He may have to sleep in the hayloft a couple more nights, but she knew he would soon make a fine little home out of this cabin.

"If you need anything to finish setting up the house just come over and we'll see what we can find at the big house," she said as she stepped out the door.

"Don't you worry, Miss Becky," he replied. "I have collected things for years in hopes I would someday have a home of my own. What little I need I could buy in town I'm sure. Josh has put me in charge of the orchards and beehives, and I will soon be as busy as those little winged critters that buzz around outside. "

Rebecca slowly walked back toward the house. She took deep breaths of the fresh mountain air, perfumed with the fragrance of flowers from the meadow.

She passed by the garden and saw there were plenty of vegetables to be harvested. There were enough beans for a couple dozen quarts and a variety of squash and pumpkins on the vines. She loaded her apron with a few tomatoes and summer squash and started toward the house as Dave pulled up with her new stove and a big copper bathtub. With a squeal of delight, she rushed to the side of the wagon and ran her hand along the smooth side of the tub. Josh approached from the barn, and she hurried toward him. A couple tomatoes escaped from her apron as she ran.

"Thank you, Josh," she said as she gave his arm a

squeeze. "I wondered how I was to bathe with only a wash pan."

Josh gave Dave a puzzled look as he went up to the wagon to see what had given her such pleasure. He turned toward the guilty-looking Dave, who quickly said, "You told me to get whatever she needed. You can't expect her to bathe in the creek like you do, now can you?"

With a blush she quickly turned and hurried into the house. Soon the men had removed the old pot-bellied stove and carried in the new cast-iron range. Dave had purchased a six-cap stove with a large oven, a warming shelf, and water storage tank that kept a supply of hot water ready at all times. As soon as they finished, Dave brought in kindling and started the first fire, then filled the reservoir with water. While the stove heated, Rebecca swept the porches and brought out a couple of odd chairs. *I wonder if Josh could make me a porch swing for next summer?* she thought to herself. She envisioned some colorful cushions scattered in the chairs and swing that would give the porch a look of welcome for visitors. Soon the men came back to the house and into the front room.

"Boss told us to take this old table over to Dave's new kitchen," said Brad, and they started to carry it out.

"But what I will use?" she asked as she looked at the bare place.

"We'll be right back. Boss said there was a table

and things stored upstairs and for us to carry down whatever you wanted."

She watched them cross to the bunkhouse. They wrestled with the heavy table as Dave scurried alongside and bossed the job. With a smile she hurried over to the stairs and opened the door, her long skirts stirring up the dust as she climbed the narrow steps. She was delighted to discover four more bedrooms with a collection of furnishings. As she heard the men stomp up the stairs she chose an oval-shaped pedestal table of oak with claw feet. Eight oak chairs with flowers and vines carved into the backs were also chosen, along with a writing table and chair she would place under the window in the living room. As soon as everything was settled downstairs, she would attempt to restore order to these bedrooms in case they had overnight guests.

Later Josh came in for a quick lunch, but before he returned to work, he sat down in the large rocker and gathered the blushing Rebecca onto his lap.

"Now what made you blush?" he said, with a twinkle in his blue eyes. "We've been married one day and I've hardly got to spend any time with my bride."

"I can barely remember my papa," she answered with a self-conscious look, "but one thing I do remember was the way he would hold Mama and me on his lap and talk over the day's events before we went to bed. It was a sweet time I will always remember. That was the time we always had our devotions from the Bible, too."

"Well, I think we will just have to continue that tradition. We'll start tonight," he said as he gave her a gentle squeeze.

"Oh, I didn't mean to hint to sit on your lap every night," she said, as her face grew warmer.

"Maybe not," he said with a chuckle, "but I still think it's a good idea. Would you like to go down to Brother Smith's church in the morning? He said the ladies always bring some dishes of food and everyone just has a picnic after the morning services. Then about two o'clock they have an afternoon service so that everyone can get home before dark. You can break in that new stove this afternoon. We'll be leaving early in the morning since it's about an hour ride by wagon to Shadow Valley." Rebecca nodded her assent, and then Josh said, "Well, as much as I'd like to stay right here all afternoon, I guess I'd better get back to work." Giving her a tender kiss, he headed out the door. She watched him walk toward the barn with a look of contentment on her face.

Dave brought in two plump hens, plucked and ready to fry. By evening she had prepared delicious fried chicken and two freshly baked apple pies with flaky crust laced with cinnamon and sugar that cooled in the window. She stepped out on the porch to hang out some dishtowels as Charlie and Dave rode by. Charlie smelled the pies and said, "I hope the Boss shares those pie with some of us hungry working men."

With a laugh, she said, "These pies are going to Shadow Valley Church early in the morning, and those who want a slice will just have to hop on the back of the wagon and go along."

Later that night, Josh pondered why some of the men hadn't rushed off to town as usual when he handed out their wages. He was surprised, but pleased, to learn that a few of the men yearned for freshly baked apple pie more than the lure of the whiskey at Boone's saloon.

Chapter Twelve

> *Six days thou shalt work, but on the seventh day thou shalt rest: in earing time and in harvest thou shalt rest.*
>
> Exodus 34:21

They arose early the next morning and had breakfast before the sun was up. Rebecca enjoyed her first bath in the big tub that Josh had filled before he went to the barn. She dressed in a blue chambray traveling suit and put her hair up in a mass of burnished curls, then pinned on a natural straw hat with blue and yellow flowers nestled around the brim.

While Josh dressed, she packed the fried chicken and pies in baskets and set them on the table, ready to be loaded in the wagon. After supper last night, Arthur had whispered to her that some of the men planned to go to church with them, so she had rushed to make a peach and three more apple pies before going to bed. She had made extra biscuits at breakfast, and three dozen lay on top of the basket of chicken.

Charlie was the first to arrive: he brought around the wagon that had been swept clean in preparation for the day. He wore a clean red and white checkered shirt and jeans, and his pale blond hair was parted in the middle and slicked down on the sides, giving him a comical look. After nervously pacing a few minutes, he disappeared toward the bunkhouse not to be seen the rest of the day.

Arthur arrived in a sparkling white shirt and his freshly pressed black suit. In his hand he carried his worn Bible and a black derby.

As Josh loaded the baskets of food into the wagon and helped Rebecca up onto the front seat, three of the men came from the bunkhouse in a variety of apparel. Dave had tried to control his mop of gray-streaked red hair to little avail. Brad wore a worn black suit and carried his Bible. Brent Bennett, who was in his early twenties, stopped by the front porch, then climbed sheepishly into the back with the rest. He wore a bright blue shirt that accentuated his azure eyes.

With extreme pride, Josh climbed up beside Rebecca, picked up the reins, and started down the road. The road to Shadow Valley was a slow decline, which made easy travel on the way down, but it would be very tiresome on the horses as well as passengers on the way back. It traveled through the aspen woods and hidden glens, across the many rambling streams that were scattered throughout the valley. Just outside the small community of Shadow Valley they came upon a newly erected church with fresh-sawed board siding and four long, narrow windows on each side. There were many wagons and horses already tied to the trees that surrounded the church, and some men set up tables made of long, rough sawed lumber. Children in their Sunday best ran and played, trying to exhaust some of their energy before services began. They knew their parents would not tolerate squirming in the pews.

Most of the people there knew Josh and his men, but very few had heard of his marriage. Rebecca was a surprise to most of them, and a disappointment to many mothers who had hopes of their daughters capturing the elusive Josh. With pride, Josh introduced her to his close friends from the surrounding ranches. They all welcomed her and made her feel as if she had known them a long time.

They sat on narrow wooden benches as Jonathan Smith preached to them from Ephesians 6:10–18. The message from these scriptures was delivered with power and wisdom. The pastor explained that their warfare was not against their brothers and sisters in Christ, but against Satan and his demonic sidekicks. Because of this warfare they must arm themselves for battle. They must have the truth of the Word of God. They must have righteousness. They were to march forward proclaiming the Gospel to the lost. And they must have faith in God and his Word. With that faith they could protect themselves from everything the devil may throw at them. They must be born again and have always the Word of God in their hearts.

Many made the decision that morning to walk closer to the Lord and to serve him more. Some made professions of faith and wished to be baptized. There were many teary eyes as the congregation filed out the door and thanked Brother Smith for the message that had stirred their hearts.

In a short time the women had the board tables dressed in tablecloths and sheets. A bounty of food soon covered the tables. The women served the men and children, then filled their own plates and joined their families on the backs of wagons or on quilts on the ground.

Rebecca sat on a quilt in the shade of their wagon while Josh relaxed against the wagon wheel. "What do you think of the church here?" he asked her.

"I like the friendliness of the people I've met," she responded, "and Brother Smith is a really sound preacher. His messages just feed your soul, and restore that desire to serve the Lord more."

"Yes, I like him better than the preacher they have in town. I believe this would be a good church in which to serve the Lord."

Everyone was quiet on the ride home, but peace was evident on the faces of Arthur and Brad, and the others seemed to be deep in thought. It had been a real experience for Brent, since his parents had never made the effort to take him to church when he was young.

Rebecca silently prayed for each of the men, that they would desire to go again to hear the Word preached, not just for the food and entertainment. The sun disappeared behind the mountains as they pulled into the yard. Josh helped a tired but happy Rebecca down from the wagon and went in to change out of his Sunday clothes. As he did the nightly chores he thought of the busy week he faced. The wheat was to be harvested and the hay brought into the barns. Before going back to the house, he made a detour up to the swimming hole for a refreshing swim.

The next two days were busy for everyone as hay was brought in and all hands needed and used. Rebecca baked bread and made sandwiches for lunch with thick slices of cold ham and plenty of cold apple cider. In the afternoon she unpacked some more of her treasures and scattered them about the house, giving it the needed woman's touch. By dark, she had a hearty supper on the table for the men, which they ate with relish and headed straight for bed.

On Wednesday the threshing machine and its crew arrived to harvest the wheat. Some of the wives of the crew always came along and helped the farmers' wives cook for and feed them. They did a lot of the cooking outside, and Arthur made board tables under the shade trees for the men to eat on.

After the threshing crew left, the wheat was hauled to the mill to be ground into flour. The men began once again to get the hay into the barns.

The next couple of months were a busy time for everyone. Rebecca canned, preserved, and dried everything she could find to harvest. Big juicy peaches were canned, apples dried, and jams and jellies made. She made a batch of apple butter in a large copper kettle outside over an open fire. With Arthur's and Dave's assistance, she made gallons of apple cider that she stored down in the cool cellar. Rebecca had always been a hard worker, but the chores and duties at the ranch were much more strenuous and back-breaking than she had been used to. The hours were long, and she went to bed each night exhausted. Josh noticed her fatigue and was concerned about her. One day he decided to take a day off from his duties.

"Honey, pack us a good lunch, and after I see that the chores are done and the men started on their work for the day, we'll head up into the hills. I know where a late berry grows that makes delicious jelly."

"Oh, Josh, that sounds like fun."

"I believe we both need a break," he smiled, giving her an affectionate hug.

After the berries had been picked, they enjoyed their lunch in a shady cove filled with delicate wild-flowers that bloomed profusely by a small stream. Josh stretched out on a quilt, gazing up through the tree branches at the blue sky. Rebecca wandered around enjoying the beauty of God's creation. It was so vastly different from the hills of West Virginia. She climbed out on a small outcrop of rocks, selecting a seat near the edge. The view of the luscious green valley was breathtaking. She could see the house in the distance. The cultivated fields of corn, hay, golden wheat stubble, and the orchard made a patchwork design on the landscape.

Thank you, God, for bringing me to this beautiful country, she silently prayed. *You have given me more than I ever dreamed possible, more than I deserve. I have a home, a loving husband, a church, and new friends. The only thing missing is children. Lord, if you see fit, I pray that you let us have a family. Children would make our marriage complete.*

She became drowsy in the warm sun and stretched out beside Josh in the shade. Soon, both were asleep.

While they slept a dark, ominous thundercloud billowed up in the west. Josh woke with a start. The dark cloud covered the sun, and flashes of lightening zigzagged across the horizon.

"Rebecca, wake up!" said Josh with concern. "We've got to get back to the house before this storm breaks."

They hurriedly gathered up the quilt, lunch basket, and the basket of berries and headed down the hill to the wagon. The team was restless and it took a tight rein to keep them from breaking into a run. Big drops of rain began to splatter around them as the storm quickly overtook them. A vicious bolt of lightening struck a tree to their left, splitting it down the center. The thunder rumbled, reverberating off the hills. When they reached a level stretch of road, Josh let the team run. The rain came down in a deluge, soaking them to the skin before they reached shelter. When they pulled into the barn, Rebecca realized they had lost the basket of berries and their leftover lunch somewhere along the way.

Charlie came from the bunkhouse with some slickers.

"Boss, I'll rub the team down for you," he said. "Put these slickers on and take the missus to the house before she gets pneumonia."

Josh and Rebecca rushed toward the house. Near the back steps she slipped in the mud and fell. Josh gathered her up in his arms and ran into the house. He set a cold, chilled Rebecca in a chair by the kitchen stove and quickly built up the fire.

"Get those wet clothes off and wrap up in this quilt," said Josh as he rushed from the bedroom with a quilt. "Hurry. This is not the time to be modest."

"But what if someone comes in?" she asked, glancing toward the door.

"No one but us would be crazy enough to get caught out in a storm like this," laughed Josh. "That's what we get for snoozing during the day."

He helped her out of the wet clothes, wrapped her in the quilt, and carried her to the bed. Stripping off his rain-soaked clothes, he laid them on the stone hearth and then climbed in beside her. It was several minutes before Rebecca could stop shivering. As the covers captured their body heat and dispelled the chill, they drifted off to sleep wrapped snugly in each other's arms.

Chapter Thirteen

Blessed are ye that hunger now: for ye shall be filled. Blessed are ye that weep now: for ye shall laugh.

Luke 6:21

The golden aspen lost their leaves as fall quietly retreated and winter's first snow blanketed the tops of the Rocky Mountains. Josh sold more of his longhorns and had moved his remaining herd to the newly fenced lower pasture closer to the barns. The inhabitants of Platte Valley had experienced some severe winters in the past and had learned it was best to be prepared for the worst. Josh was able to spend more time around the house and was getting a good supply of firewood stacked on the porches and the woodshed filled. Rebecca had discovered a sewing machine stored upstairs. She now had crisp, ruffled curtains of muslin on all the windows and was skillfully piecing on a quilt and patchwork pillows in the evenings by the fire. Josh enjoyed sitting by the huge stone fireplace where its flames imparted a cheerful glow while he read or worked on some small project. He also enjoyed watching Rebecca work, and with love in his eyes, silently thanked God for his blessings. His appreciation to his older brother Matt for his wisdom concerning Rebecca filled his heart.

When Sunday arrived, they bundled up and headed for Shadow Valley, knowing it would probably be their last trip to fellowship with their brethren until spring. Arthur and Brad had been faithful to attend almost every service, and Josh planned to start a Bible study on Sundays during the long, cold winter months and welcome all the men for fellowship and a good dinner.

As they drove up to church, they espied a young girl grasping the hand of a small boy as they hurried toward the building. Rebecca couldn't help but notice the matted hair and dirty face of the scantily clad boy. The girl also had an unkempt appearance, but she had endeavored to pull her dirty hair back and tie it with a piece of string, and her thin face was reasonably clean. Neither child had on a coat. Rebecca knew they had to be almost frozen. She herself was chilled even with her heavy woolen cloak and quilts bundled around her. *I wonder where their parents are and why the children look so neglected,* Rebecca thought.

All during the service, the children hugged close to the potbellied stove that stood in the center aisle of the church. No one seemed to pay any attention to them, but Rebecca couldn't keep her eyes from straying toward them.

After services the men lit big bonfires, and the women put on huge pots of coffee and spread the food on the tables. The two children ate ravenously as if they hadn't had a decent meal in days. Rebecca saw the small boy slyly stuff biscuits and chicken into his dirty pants pocket when he thought no one was watching.

Hank, a big, rough-looking man, suddenly grabbed the small boy by the shirt collar and yelled, "Why, you sneaking little thief, you ain't got no business here stealin' decent folk's food! You go on home where ye belong and stay there."

As he gave the frightened boy a rough push away from the table, a wildcat of a girl jumped on his back, pulling his hair, clawing and yelling, "You leave my brother alone! We got just as much right here as ye do. He ain't hurting nobody a'tall. Especially an old goat like you!"

Brother Smith heard the disturbance and came over, gently leading the angered girl away to where her small brother stood sobbing.

"Rachael, you shouldn't fight the man like that, even if he is wrong. You and your brother go ahead and eat, and I'll have a talk with him." He smiled at the boy and gave the girl a reassuring pat on the shoulder before he turned and walked toward the man.

The girl gathered the small boy in her arms and, looking defiantly back at the crowd, turned away and started down the road.

Rebecca, not being able to stand it any longer, went over to the pastor with concern in her eyes.

"Brother Smith," she said with a slight quiver in her voice, "who are those children? Where are their parents?"

"They haven't any," he answered with a sigh. "Their mother died four years ago when the boy was born. The girl has done the best she could to raise him from a baby. Their father hasn't been seen for several months. He has a bad drinking habit and is known to beat the kids when he comes home drunk, but he's never stayed away this long. I'm concerned that something has happened to him."

"But where do they live?" she asked as Josh came up to her side. "Are they staying with someone?"

"No," replied Jonathan. "Rachael is real independent and doesn't want any handouts, as she calls them. She has such a temper no one wants to cross her. They live in a shack up the valley and barely get by when their father is around. I don't know what they are doing for food, but they always show up at the free feedings. They walked about eight miles to get here this morning."

With tears in her eyes, Rebecca turned and looked down the road as the despondent little figures trudged along in the cold.

"Don't worry, Little One," Josh said, slipping his arm around her small waist and giving her a comforting squeeze, "They're in God's hands and he will provide."

But during the next two days her mind kept

returning to the children and wondering how they were. When she was cooking, she worried that they might be hungry; or lying in her warm bed, she wondered if they were warm.

Josh had planned on one more trip to town for winter supplies, and since the weather was mild, he asked Rebecca if she wanted to go along. She did need a few things and also wanted to purchase some material to make Josh some new shirts for winter. She went to her trunk to get some money she had saved. Josh knew about the money her father had left her and had told her to keep it for things she needed to buy.

As they arrived in town, Rebecca gasped as she saw the man Hank head toward the sheriff's office, dragging a girl along roughly while the boy hung on to her skirt, crying.

"Josh, stop!" she cried, grabbing his arm. "What's he doing to them?"

As Josh pulled the team over, Sheriff Callahan walked out to see what the commotion was about.

"Sheriff," Hank said as he pulled the girl roughly up on the sidewalk, "I caught this gal stealing my food this morning and I want somethin' done."

"I didn't steal none of your old food!" she screamed. She kicked and tried to pull away from his bruising grip. "Sheriff, you gotta believe me. I can't go to jail, 'cause I gotta take care of my little brother!"

"Now, take it easy, Missy," the sheriff said. He looked at Hank. "Turn her loose. She ain't going nowhere."

"Sheriff, I don't want no trouble, but if you can find someone to look after the boy there, I'll just take this gal home with me and she can work out what she stole." Glancing at the girl, he was not able to hide the lust in his eyes. "I be needin' someone to cook for me anyhow, now that my woman up and died."

"Oh, Josh, no," gasped Rebecca in a whisper, "she can't go live with that evil man. Can't you see what's on his mind? She's just a child!"

"Now you just stay out of this, Holt," said Hank angrily, casting a resentful look at Rebecca, "This ain't none of you and your missus' business."

"I just wanted to ask the girl what she stole from you," he said, with a questioning look toward the girl, who was bravely hiding her fear.

"She didn't steal nothin' from that old goat," spoke up the little boy in defense of his sister. "That old bee tree weren't even on his property. Belonged to Mr. Carey!"

Josh turned to the angry man. "You mean she was just getting honey from a tree that wasn't even on your property?"

"That honey belonged to me. I been watchin' that tree all summer, waitin' for them bees to go in for the winter. She hant got no right gettin' that there honey," Hank argued, reaching out to grasp at the girl again. "Somethin' gotta be done about these brats before they start stealin' from everyone."

Rebecca had climbed down from the wagon and quietly stepped up beside Josh.

"I know you said God would make a way for them

to be taken care of," she whispered to Josh, "but he's laid it on my heart that we're the way. They wouldn't be any trouble, and I can buy them new clothes with the money I have saved. You know the Lord has blessed us with a bountiful harvest," she continued, looking up at him with pleading eyes, "and I am sure he will continue to bless us if we do his will. It would just be until their father is located."

With a tender smile he gave her a nod of approval. She was proving to be very much like his mother, always sacrificing herself for others.

Rebecca stepped over to the small boy and gently put her arm around his bony shoulder. Not to frighten him, she whispered, "I don't have a little boy at my house to take care of this winter and I was wondering if you would care to stay there until your father comes home?"

He looked up with yearning at his sister, who eyed Rebecca suspiciously. He said sadly, "I hav'ta stay with Rachael 'cause she wouldn't have nobody to take care of her."

"But I want you both to come," said Rebecca, with a smile toward Rachael, "because I know a brother and sister shouldn't be separated. I'm afraid that might happen if someone isn't willing to take you both."

"I know what ye gettin' at Ma'am, but we don't want to be no trouble to nobody," Rachael mumbled.

"But you won't be any trouble where you are truly wanted and loved. Won't you please come?"

"Well, just for a few days till Pa gets home," she reluctantly replied, remembering her little brother as he had shivered in the cold shack that morning.

"Then that's settled," said the sheriff, with a smile at the little boy who looked up at Rebecca with excitement in his eyes.

"Now, wait just a minute," shouted Hank, who realized he had just been cheated out of a cook and housekeeper, "I want—"

"The sheriff said it's settled," interrupted Josh, giving the man a look that caused him to take a step back, "and he's the law! Hop into the wagon, folks. Let's go get some breakfast." He gently picked up the small boy and set him on his shoulder, carrying him to the back of the wagon, where Rachael quickly climbed in beside him, protectively.

As they drove down the street toward Molly's boarding house, Rebecca looked at Josh and smiled a thank you. They didn't talk a whole lot, but they had learned to read each other's expressions and knew exactly what was on each other's minds and in each other's hearts.

"What's your name, son?" asked Josh, as they waited for their food to be served.

"Levi," he answered, softly, with a grin on his dusty face. "My ma named me from the Good Book, just 'fore she died."

"That's a good name," smiled Rebecca, "and Rachael is a Bible name, too. Your mother must have enjoyed reading her Bible."

"Yeah," replied Rachael, with a sad look in her

eyes. "Except when Pa was home. He didn't like her to read the Book. Said she'd turn into a self-righteous old bat like her ma. I never got to see my grandma, but Ma said she was a real kind woman. I think Ma must have been like her."

Just then the food arrived and all was quiet while the eggs, sausage, and hotcakes quickly disappeared.

When everyone had had their fill, Rebecca said to Josh, "Why don't you take Levi with you while Rachael and I go over to the mercantile and buy what we need?"

"Sounds great! Come on, Son," he said, taking Levi's small hand in his. "Be back in about an hour, ladies." As they went through the door, Levi smiled from ear to ear, looking up proudly at his new idol.

At the store, Rebecca quickly put on the counter what she had on her list, then headed over to the clothing and chose pants and a shirt in Levi's size.

"Is this the right size for your brother?" she asked holding up the soft gray pants and the blue flannel shirt.

"We don't want no handouts, Ma'am," she replied, with pride in her eyes.

Feeling exasperation at the girl's stubbornness, she turned back to the counter.

"You and your brother will have chores to do, and a lot of them will be outside, so I want you warmly dressed. If you should get sick, Josh says there's no way to get a doctor to the ranch during snows. So, how about this coat?" she said, turning with a warm smile on her face, her emotions under control.

"Ma'am, if you mean we can work them out, that's all right, but I don't need nothin' 'cause I ain't never sick."

Not wanting to anger the young girl, she secretly purchased a set of underclothes and some extra lengths of material to make her some dresses. Since she had never attempted to make little boys' clothes, she added another outfit in brown for Levi.

She had just paid for her purchases when Levi ran through the door like a tornado and headed straight for the glass candy jars.

"You get away from there, kid," hollered the storekeeper, rushing over to the candy counter.

"My boy just wants to buy some candy, Sir," said Josh as he stepped up to the counter and handed Levi two pennies. "Pick out what you want, Son, and pay the man."

"Sorry Josh, I didn't know the kid was with you," he said nervously, knowing what a good customer Josh was, especially when it came to paying his bill.

"You shouldn't treat any boy like that, even if he wasn't a paying customer," replied Josh, as he walked away from the counter loaded down with packages.

Rachael looked away quickly to hide the tears in her eyes. No one had ever stood up for her little brother in all of his four years, except herself. Her respect for Josh increased because of his kindness.

With the wagon loaded, they headed back toward the ranch. A cold, bitter wind had started to blow down from the mountains and Rebecca handed a quilt to Rachael. She and her brother wrapped up snugly, and Levi soon fell asleep.

As they came in sight of the house, Rachael and Levi looked with astonishment down in the valley at what Josh had said was home. Rachael had never seen such a large house out in the countryside, and Levi wriggled with excitement at the barns and buildings he could explore.

When they pulled up in front of the house, Charlie was waiting, and with a surprised look at the extra cargo, he quickly lifted the boy down, keeping his dismay well hidden. He turned to assist the girl, but she had already climbed down and hurried around to the other side, casting a frightened look back at him. There was not one of her pa's friends she could trust, and it made her leery of all men.

Rebecca saw the frightened look, took Rachael's arm, and hurried into the house.

Chapter Fourteen

As the purchases were brought in, the children sat nervously on the edges of their chairs, looking around with wonder. The masculine look of the house had been toned down with just a few womanly touches. Some knickknacks caught Levi's eye.

He started to get up and look around, but Rachael grabbed his arm and whispered sternly, "Sit down and don't you touch nothin'." Glancing up, she caught Josh watching them with laughter in his eyes. "Ain't nothin' safe when Brother is around," she said with a sigh as she glanced around at all the pretty knickknacks.

"Don't fret, little lady," he said, "he'll soon learn that when he wants to play rough, he can go to the barn. We have a cat that has hidden her kittens somewhere in the hayloft and they will soon be ready to come out and play."

"Oh boy, can I go find them?" he yelled, running to the door.

"No, Son, you must wait for me to show you around the first time. There are some places that are not safe and you will not be allowed there. Come help me with the rest of the packages and then we'll go together."

When everything had been carried in, Rebecca pulled out the new coat and handed it to him. Hugging the soft, warm material to his chest, he looked up at her with big tears in his eyes.

"I ain't never had nothin' so warm and beautiful," he whispered. "You can bet I'll be the best boy in the whole state of Colorado."

Rebecca quickly turned and went into the small bedroom so no one could see her tears. She had put the things she bought for the children on the bed where they would sleep. Feeling someone's presence, she turned to find Rachael watching her with a questioning expression. Gathering the little ragamuffin in her arms gently, so as not to embarrass her, she said, "It feels so good to have someone that's thankful for something as simple as a coat. And I have something for you, too. But first, we are going to fill my big tub with hot water and you can have a leisurely bath while the men are at the barn." She put her arm around the slender waist and led Rachael to the tub. "You just go behind that screen and slip out of your clothes while I get the water."

As she hesitated, Rebecca gave her an encouraging smile.

"I ain't never had no tub bath," Rachael said nervously. "Me and Ma always took our wash in the crik."

"Once is all it takes and you'll never want to bathe in that cold, icy water again," Rebecca said with a laugh. "Now, hurry."

With the tub almost full of hot, sudsy water, Rachael ventured into the water, sighing with pleasure. Rebecca came in with a soft fluffy towel and some shampoo.

"Can I help wash your hair?" she asked, as she laid out new underclothes on the bed. "It makes me feel like a new woman when I wash my hair," she said with a smile.

Rachael allowed Rebecca to shampoo and rinse her hair. In her closet she found a dress that had become too short for her, but because her mother had made it for her she couldn't bear to part with it. She thought it would fit the girl until she could make her some clothes.

"How old are you and your brother?"

"I'll be fourteen in December," she said, "and Levi will be four the same day. Ma said he was my boy, 'cause he was born on my birthday. I think she knew she was gonna die. Levi was just two days old when she died. It was the day 'fore Christmas and I ain't never had another happy Christmas."

"I know how hard it was to give up my mother, and I know it had to be terrible for a young girl left to take care of a newborn baby. But I think you have done a good job taking care of your brother. So, your birthdays are on the twenty-second? We will have a big celebration, for sure!"

Rebecca was surprised at Rachael's age. She was on the verge of womanhood, yet still had the look of a child because of her undernourished body.

She stepped out of the room while the girl dried and put on the soft new underclothes. Rachael had never seen clothes this fancy. She had always crudely stitched up any clothes she had out of scraps of material. She then put on the periwinkle blue dress and black leather slippers that Rebecca had found in the trunk. She was looking in the full-length mirror, feeling like a princess, when Rebecca returned. The color of the dress turned her blue eyes to a violet color, and her hair was curly and dark as a crow's wing. With so much dust built up in her hair, Rebecca hadn't realized the blackness of it. She would turn into a beautiful young woman in the next few years. Not wanting to build her pride up in her looks, Rebecca just gave her an admiring smile and handed her a clean white apron to put on.

"We must get supper ready before our two hungry men get back from the barn. Will you peel the potatoes while I make the biscuits? I baked a ham before going to town this morning, so it won't take long to have supper on the table," she said as she hurried to the kitchen.

The girl pleasantly went about her work, occasionally casting admiring glances at the sparkling clean kitchen and into the front room.

Soon a tired but excited Levi burst into the room and shouted, "Josh said I could have a puppy if I fed it myself and kept it in the barn. I told him Mr. Carey had some new ones."

"Well, let's have supper and we'll see," laughed Rebecca. "Josh, you show Levi where to wash his hands for supper," she said as she noticed him staring at his sister with big eyes and a lopsided grin. Josh also wore a pleased look at her appearance.

They gathered around the table and as Josh bowed his head, Rachael and Levi cast a surprised look his way and then quickly bowed theirs. They hadn't asked the blessing on the food in town because both of the children had been so hungry they had started eating as soon as the plates were set in front of them, and Josh hadn't wanted to embarrass them.

When supper was over, the women cleaned off the table and washed the dishes, while Josh showed Levi where the kindling was and how to fill the box by the stove. He then carried some buckets of hot water to the tub, and soon Rachael had stripped the dirty clothes off the skinny frame of her little brother and gave him his first tub bath, much to his delight. Rebecca brought him some new long johns for him to sleep in and quietly gathered up the smelly clothes and carried them to the back porch.

They sat around the fire, and Josh reverently picked up his Bible and said to the new family members, "The Lord has blessed us so much in our lifetime, and today he has added another blessing by bringing you to live with us for a while. We want you to feel this is your home, and if you have a need for anything, come let us know. Because the Lord loves us so much, we like to spend a little time each evening reading his Word and thanking him for his many blessings. I hope you both will always have the desire to join us each evening before going to bed."

After the Bible reading, Josh carried the sleepy Levi to bed in a room that he and Rachael would share. The room looked stark and bare compared to the rest of the house, but Rebecca planned to fix it up like any young girl would like, even if she did have to share it with her little brother.

Later, as Rebecca lay snuggled in her husband's arms, she said, "Josh, thank you for letting them come to live with us. I have been so concerned about them ever since I saw them at church. I couldn't seem to keep my mind on my work. And Rachael will be a great help to me." Looking up at Josh with eyes full of love, she said, "I think we are going to have a baby of our own, come summer."

"A baby? You're going to have my baby?" he asked with wonder in his eyes. "Oh, Honey, you make me so proud. Just wait until Matt gets here. He won't have anything on me—with his three kids," he laughed, then sadly added, "But we must remember that their father may show up anytime to claim them."

"I know. I try not to think about it happening, at least not 'til we get them fattened up and clothed."

They drifted off to sleep with smiles on their faces and contentment in their hearts.

Chapter Fifteen

Giving thanks always for all things
unto God and the Father in the name
of our Lord Jesus Christ;

Ephesians 5:20

The next morning, after the chores were done and a wash had been hung out in the breeze to dry, Rebecca and the children headed toward the little cabin out back to be introduced to Arthur. Levi skipped here and there in the crisp winter breeze while Rachael walked beside Rebecca, smiling at her brother's antics.

Arthur had settled in for the winter like an old groundhog after a busy fall. He had pruned all the fruit trees and robbed the bees of their excess honey, which he had put in jars for Josh to trade in town. He had also planted flower bulbs and rose cuttings around the cabin. He and Rebecca planned to make some flowerbeds around the main house in the spring. Close to the gurgling stream that wandered by the cabin was a wildflower garden that held many different vines and delicate flowers that the Daniels' children had gathered in the woods when they lived there. These were all snuggled dormant in the ground, waiting for the warm spring rains.

Arthur answered the door, holding a ball of rag strips in his hand. He was in the process of making some small, braided rag rugs to match the one that covered a large area of his cabin. The cabin had a warm, cozy look and smelled of freshly baked bread. A fire danced in the huge rock fireplace, its flames imparting a cheerful glow to the chinked log walls.

"Well, who is this fine fellow?" he asked, patting Levi on his head of tousled brown curls, while nodding to the solemn girl standing by his Miss Becky.

"This is Levi and his sister Rachael. They have to come to stay with us for a while. We wanted to come up and remind you that next week is Thanksgiving, and we want you and all the men to have dinner with us. Brent has his eye on a flock of turkeys, and I told him we would need two to feed this hungry crew."

"You can count on me, Miss Becky," he smiled. "I'm getting a little tired of my own company, and the snow hasn't even started."

"Don't worry, Mr. Arthur," piped in Levi, "I'll come see you every day so you won't get lonesome. And when I get my puppy he'll come with me, too."

"A puppy?" Arthur was amused at the proud look on the boy's face. "That's just what our flower beds will need in the spring," he winked at Rebecca.

Arthur took Levi around the room, showing what he called his treasures. Some weapons and a uniform from the Civil War, a collection of arrowheads and tomahawks, a peace pipe, and a string of stone beads. Seeing that Rachael was intrigued with how the rug was being braided, Rebecca told her she could start one, after Thanksgiving, to put in her room. This would help her to pass the long winter hours. *It is going to be nice to have another female in the house, no matter how young.*

They wandered back toward the house, stopping at the chicken coop.

"Rachael, it will be your chore to care for the chickens. The feed is kept in these wooden kegs. Be sure to put the lids back on when you finish, or the mice will have a feast. They will have to be watered twice a day when the weather drops to freezing."

They strolled over to the lot by the barn where Josh and Charlie worked with some horses. One was a dapple-gray mare that Josh was breaking for Rebecca, but now, with the baby on the way, she wouldn't be able to ride it until next summer. Levi climbed the fence and sat straddling the top rail, pretending he was riding a wild bronco. As Rebecca leaned on the rail fence watching her husband work-ing with the mare, she admired the way his shirt fit snugly across his muscled back and the way he kept his black hair out of his eyes with a bandana tied Indian-style around his head.

Turning to look at Rachael, who was standing timidly by her side, she asked, "Do you know how to ride?"

"I've rode Pa's old work mule some, but he

wouldn't never let me on his horse. That horse had a nasty streak in 'im sometimes."

"If you would like to learn, we'll ask Josh to teach you. That's my horse he is working with. Her name is Pepper. I can't wait to ride her, but I won't be able to for a while, so maybe you could learn to ride and take care of her."

"But, why can't ya ride her?" she asked, looking nervously at the mare.

"Well, this will be our secret. Josh is the only one I've told so far. I'm going to have a baby next summer," she said with a happy smile. "I am so happy, but a little nervous, too. I was the only child my parents had, and I always wished I could have a big family. That's why I am so pleased you and Levi are staying with us."

"I'll 'elp you real good, so you won't get too tired," Rachael said with a worried look. "I think Ma worked too hard before Levi was born, and I don't want ya to get sick like her."

"Oh, Rachael, I'm real strong and healthy, and I won't have any trouble," she said, giving the girl a hug. "Don't you worry about me. I'm sure by the time spring comes I'll be glad to have you around, though."

Josh came over leading Pepper. "Well, ladies," he said, placing his hand lovingly over Rebecca's. "What do you think of her?" He looked at the mare with pride.

"She's beautiful!" said Rachael as she reached cautiously to caress the soft, gray nose. "She said I might learn to ride 'er," she added, glancing at Rebecca.

"Sure! We can start next week and soon you'll be out herding the cattle with the men," he said with a laugh. Rachael looked nervously at Charlie and smiled weakly.

Josh handed the reins over to Charlie and headed to the house for lunch. Rebecca called to Charlie, "You tell the men they are invited to eat Thanksgiving dinner next week."

"Ma'am, that's all Dave talks about," said Charlie with a grin. "He just sits 'round and drools, thinkin' of your delicious apple pie and all the other goodies you make. I thought he was gonna tackle poor little Levi when he came in the barn this mornin' eating one of your big oatmeal cookies."

With a laugh, Rebecca hurried to the kitchen and fixed cold ham sandwiches and dished up big, steaming bowls of potato soup while Josh and Levi washed up. After they left, she showed Rachael the quilt she was making and soon both were busy talking and getting acquainted as they worked.

It suddenly dawned on Rebecca that it had been quiet for too long a time. She turned to Rachael and said, "You'd better check on your brother. It's not like him to stay away from the cookie jar this long."

With a laugh, she hurried out, calling loudly, "Levi! Levi, where you at, boy? You better answer me if you know what's good for you." She got no answer so she hurried around the house and was headed toward Arthur's when she heard him sob. She found him on the roof of the smokehouse rubbing his teary eyes with his grimy little fists. Dave had been patching the roof and had left the ladder standing when he'd finished. Not many four-year-old boys can resist climbing a ladder, so he had scrambled up on the roof, knocking the ladder over in the process and leaving himself stranded. She ran over and climbed up to rescue him when he began to cry even harder.

"Levi, what's wrong? Are you hurt?" she asked, starting to get worried.

"Miss Becky gonna send me away," he bellowed. "She got me these new pants and I tored 'em." He sat with his hand over the hole and his skinned knee, sobbing.

"Now Little Brother, you know better'n that. I bet she can patch them quick as a wink. You just crawl over 'ere and I'll help you down." When she had him safely on the ground, she said, "Now, let's go show Miss Becky, but don't you worry none."

They both had started calling Rebecca "Miss Becky" after their visit to Arthur's. Rebecca was glad they had found a name they were comfortable with.

"Miss Becky," he said with a sniff as he came in the door, "I done tored my new pants, but you can fix 'em, can't ya?"

With a smile, she picked him up and set him on the table. "I'm more concerned with this skinned knee than the pants. Let's slip these off and let me wash that knee and put some salve on it. Then you go in and lay on your bed and rest while I darn these pants."

He was soon asleep, exhausted from play. His undernourished body was still weak. When the pants were finished, she laid them on the bed and, leaning over, she kissed his curls and whispered, "I love you, Little Levi."

⸻

The days passed quickly, and the first snow arrived. The next day was Thanksgiving, and the house was filled with the aroma of goodies being prepared for the feast. Brent brought in two young turkeys, cleaned, plucked, and ready to bake.

Josh entered the house with an armload of wood, stomping the snow from his feet. "Looks like we're going to get a good one tonight," he said as he put the load in the woodbin and turned to take Rebecca in his arms. "Get what you need from the cellar and smokehouse and have Levi bring in extra kindling and stack it behind the stove. Rachael should lock the chickens up and give them extra grain. It may be several days before she can get out to them if we get any big drifts."

"Josh, is it really going to get that bad?" asked Rebecca. "What about dinner tomorrow?"

"Don't worry about the men getting here," he said with a laugh. "They are getting the rope out now to tie between the barn and house."

"Rope?" she asked with a confused look.

"Yes, sometimes the winds blow the snow so hard, you can't see your hand in front of your face. We have to keep an eye on the stock, so we tie ropes between the bunkhouse and barn so the men can hold on and not get lost in the snow. Men have been found frozen just steps away from shelter because they got turned around in the blowing snow. They are running the rope to the house too, so if there are blizzard conditions tomorrow, they won't miss out on your good cooking."

"I'm not used to snow before Christmas," she said. Turning his collar up around his neck, she gave him a kiss. "You stay warm out there."

"Don't worry, Dumplin'," he said with a grin and gave her a quick hug. "Just put on a big pot of coffee. We're going to move the herd up to the lots by the barn before the snow starts so we can keep an eye on them."

He opened the door and Dave staggered in with a load of firewood. As he laid the wood on the stone hearth, he said, "Sorry, Ma'am, about the mess, but you'll need all the wood you can get to keep the fires going the next few days." He made trip after trip until each hearth was stacked high with wood.

By evening the snow was falling in big, fluffy flakes. As the wind picked up, the flakes became little pellets of ice that stung as they hit the face. The sleet left a crust on top of the snow that crunched under the feet of the men as they went about their chores. By nightfall, the soft, fluffy snow had returned. The wind howled with a vengeance as it swept down from the Rockies, swirling and twisting the snow as it maneuvered its way across the valley, driving man and beast to shelter. The cattle mingled into a circle, faces turned in, and ready to brave the fierce storm that nature had released.

The blizzard conditions continued all through the night, and the snow piled in deep drifts halfway up the windows. The next morning the men, unable to get the door of the bunkhouse open, helped Brent out the window. They handed him a shovel, and he cleared away the snow from the door. They soon had paths to all the buildings and were checking the stock as Josh came from the house.

"I hope the Missus has those turkeys in the oven, Boss," shouted Charlie, as he saw Josh approach.

"She was up and down all night basting those birds and feeding the fires," he replied. "As I left she was up to her elbows in flour, so I don't believe anyone will go hungry today."

Rebecca and Rachael bustled around the kitchen all morning and by noon, everyone was gathered around the table. Levi had worried all morning, afraid that Arthur wouldn't be able to make it from his cabin in the deep snow. He soon gave a squeal of delight as he saw him walking across the snow on a pair of snowshoes.

Thanks were offered for the food and the many blessings that God had given unto them. With their appetites satisfied, the men sprawled around in the chairs and on the floor by the fire, stuffed like the turkeys they had just devoured. Dave had brought his fiddle, and soon a melody was flowing through the room and feet began to pat in time with the music. He played every song and ditty he knew, and then ended with hymns, everyone joining in on the ones they knew.

The afternoon passed quickly and just at dark, the wind started to howl, letting the men know they had better take care of the stock and get to shelter.

After the food was put away and the dishes washed, they gathered by the fire and had their devotions. After the children went to bed, Rebecca sat snuggled on Josh's lap as they talked about the wonderful day they had enjoyed.

Chapter Sixteen

And I find more bitter than death the woman, whose heart is snares and nets, and her hands as bands...

Ecclesiastes 7:26a

In one of the elegant bedrooms of the Spanish-style house on the Double L Ranch, Cassandra Lopez paced angrily, tapping a quirt impatiently against the leather of her riding boot. The petite beauty of Spanish descent was not accustomed to being outdone by anyone without retaliation. She had arrived late last night for the Christmas festivities from an elite finishing school for women in Boston. As soon as she was alone in her room, her younger sister had smugly told her of Josh's marriage. She had received plenty of offers for marriage, but only Joshua Holt had resisted her charm, making her determined to bring him to his knees. The last time she had seen Josh had been at the Fourth of July celebration in Longmont when he had spurned her advances. She had left early the following morning for Boston, not realizing Josh was to be married that very next day.

There was a break in the winter weather, and she was determined to ride over and face the upstart who had cheated her out of her coveted role while she had been away. One of the men from the stable brought Diablo, her favorite horse, around to the front of the house and helped her mount. He was ordered by her father to accompany her. She rode off recklessly, soon leaving her escort behind as she drove her mount ruthlessly, sparing not her quirt.

Her lathered horse slowed to a walk as she approached the One Jolt Ranch. Rebecca was busy in the kitchen preparing a birthday cake for Levi and Rachael. She had heard someone walk across the porch and was headed toward the door, when suddenly it flew open and a whirlwind of anger exploded upon the scene.

"So, you're the sneaky spinster that thought she could take my man!" Cassandra spit out at the astonished Rebecca. "Joshua Holt is mine, so you might as well pack your bags and leave."

"I don't know what you are talking about, but you are the one who had better leave!" exclaimed Rebecca as she recovered from her shock.

"No! It was always meant for Josh and me to marry, and no redheaded shrew can just waltz in here, marry my man, and get away with it," she replied, striking Rebecca on the shoulder with the quirt.

In a flash, Rebecca's anger enabled her to snatch the quirt from the surprised attacker, and reply with sarcastic sweetness, "Oh, but I'm just his mail-order bride since there wasn't anyone suitable in this area to marry." She was ready to avenge when Josh walked through the door.

"What is going on here!" he shouted, seeing his wife with a whip raised above her head, aimed at a woman crouched in front of her.

She dropped her hand to her side as the woman whirled and threw herself at the astonished Josh. He tried to escape her grasp as she clung to him and sobbed. Rebecca had had about all she could take and gave a resounding whack with the quirt to the plump buttocks of the clinging woman. Cassandra let out a shriek of pain and anger as she turned with fire in her eyes. She was stopped short by the whip pointed in her face, as an angry Rebecca quietly said, "You keep your hands off my man, get out of my house, and don't ever show your face around here again. Do you hear me? And since you know how this feels," she said, holding up the quirt before tossing it in the fire, "I'm sure you won't want to use it again."

The weeping woman turned to plead with Josh, but saw his eyes dancing with laughter, and she said angrily, "You're laughing now, but it wasn't laughter I saw in your eyes last summer when we lay in the hay-loft. Remember Papa's barbecue?" Then she rushed from the house, bumping into her escort, who tried to hide his snicker at seeing his boss lady get her just reward.

Before they were out of sight, Josh was doubled over, whooping with laughter as he remarked, "I should have had you here years ago to handle that hard-headed, aggravating female." His laughter stopped short when he saw his angry spouse, hands on her hips, glaring at him.

"What are you laughing at!" she said, trying to control her anger. "I get attacked by one of your lady friends and you think it's funny. Just look at what she did to me!" she exclaimed, untying the front of her dress and, slipping it off her shoulder, she exposed the angry red welt across her creamy white shoulder and slight swell of her breast.

"She actually struck you!" he exclaimed, gently touching the welt. "Why, that shrew! I'm sorry, Honey, for laughing. I didn't know she had struck you. I only saw the funny part, especially that lick you gave her fat backside." As he tried to hide his mirth, she soon joined him; she had a nature that wouldn't let her stay angry very long. He gathered her in his arms, gently kissing her bruised shoulder, face, and honey sweet lips.

"Oh, Josh, that wasn't a very Christian way to act, was it?" she whispered. "I'm so ashamed I let my temper take control."

With a grin, he said, "I thought I had just imagined that show of temper at Molly's when you first arrived."

"Oh, hush!" she smiled, giving him a push away. "I'd better check my cake. If that woman made me burn my cake she'll get another dose of my temper." She paused and looked back at Josh. "Did she really satisfy you more than I do?" she asked with tears in her eyes.

"Honey, don't give her another thought. She offered her free kisses, and being only a man, I took all she offered to a point, but we were never intimate. You are my life now and I have no desire for anyone but you." He gathered her once again into his arms and kissed her deeply, leaving her breathless.

Josh headed out the door while she rushed to the kitchen and rescued the cake just in time, setting it out to cool. It was to be a special three layer chocolate cake with chocolate icing. All the men were coming over after supper to have cake and watch Rachael and Levi open their gifts. Josh had carved a stick horse for Levi, and she had made it a yarn mane. For Rachael, she had made a rose pink dress with big, puffed sleeves, and she had trimmed the collar with hand-crocheted lace.

After supper, she took Levi and dressed him in new black knickers and a white shirt, then appointed Josh to keep him clean until time for the party. Then she took Rachael to her room and gave her the dress so she could wear it at the party.

Rachael looked at Rebecca with tears in her eyes and said, "It's the most beautiful dress I've ever seen. I'm almost afraid to put it on 'cause I just know Levi will get something on it." Rebecca helped her slip it over her head, fasten it up the back, and then pull back her raven hair with a matching bow. There was a mature look about the girl over the last month thanks to a steady diet of wholesome food. She had filled out in all the right places, showing that she was on the verge of womanhood. Arthur had helped her and Levi with their lessons in the evenings, especially grammar, and her speech had improved.

They heard the men coming in, but Rachael hung back. She was too timid to walk out in front of the men, so Rebecca left her to come out on her own. Rebecca was pouring coffee and getting ready to serve the cake when she saw her ease from the room, quietly taking a seat near the fire.

The men had learned to approach Rachael gently and had gained her trust and respect, but they knew she was still timid around them. She had become friends with Arthur and could take teasing from him, although she was always quick to dish it back.

"Miss Becky," Arthur said in a loud whisper, "don't look now, but I think we have a visiting angel. I've never seen anything this beautiful, so it must be an angel."

"Oh, Arthur!" laughed the girl. "You're sure full of blarney tonight."

The men all joined in with their own flattery, and Brent made it a point to see that he got to serve the birthday girl her cake. Josh had bought her a gold locket in town and as soon as it was presented, all the men brought out their gifts to give to her and Levi. She received a lace handkerchief from Arthur, some cologne from Dave, chocolates from Brent, a book from Brad, and a very detailed carving of a colt from Charlie.

Levi was elated over a pair of fancy cowboy

boots that the men had pitched in together to buy along with several bags of candy. Before long he was stomping around the room in his new boots, riding his stick horse with his mouth stuffed full of candy.

When everyone had their fill of cake, Dave once again got out his fiddle and began to play. After a couple of snappy ditties, he played a slow waltz, and Brent boldly asked Rachael to dance. She surprised them all when she accepted. Not to be outdone, Josh took Rebecca by the hand and waltzed her around the room until she was breathless.

Rebecca was trying to get her wind back when Charlie casually asked, "Was that the high and mighty Miss Lopez I saw riding away like a whirlwind today?"

"It sure was!" said Josh, with a chuckle, ignoring the warning look from his spouse's eyes. "But you can be sure she'll never set foot on this ranch again. She came to conquer and went away with her tail tucked between her legs like a whipped cur. She'll know better than to mess with my little woman again." To everyone's enjoyment, he gave the full details of the episode, causing Rebecca to squirm with embarrassment as they applauded her conquest.

The evening came to a close with Dave playing hymns to go to sleep by. After the men left, Rebecca managed to get Levi settled down and headed toward bed. He knew that Christmas was just three days away, and he was sure to have many more gifts to open.

Rachael gathered up her treasures and gave

Rebecca and Josh each a hug. "This 'ere is the best birthday I have ever had in my whole life. Thank you for lovin' Levi and me and givin' us a home. It's not just the gifts, but the love you show us that makes me so happy."

The next day, Rebecca and Rachael were busy all morning making special goodies for Christmas and getting down the tree decorations Rebecca had found stored upstairs. Josh and Levi left after lunch to find the perfect tree. Rebecca moved some chairs around and created a special place for it. After supper, everyone helped string popcorn and cranberry garland to place on the tree.

Christmas Day was a joyful time, with much gift giving, delicious food, and giving of thanks. Josh took down the Bible and read the account of Christ's birth from the Book of Matthew, explaining the true meaning of the Christmas season. Everyone took part in the festivities and helped clean up afterwards.

The year of 1892 came in with another big snow, and everyone hugged close to the warm, crackling fires, finding various ways of entertainment. The children spent much of their time reading, studying, and playing games. They had received writing tablets, drawing paper, and even some watercolors for Christmas, and Rebecca saw that they put them to good use.

———◆———

In late January another blizzard swept down from the Rockies. The heavy, wet snow and ice bowed low the branches of the trees and shrubs. Many of the limbs split and broke, and the roof of the corncrib collapsed under the weight of the heavy snow.

Rebecca stood at the kitchen window washing dishes. The storm had abated earlier, and the sun reflected off the brilliant snow. Suddenly she noticed a dark figure stumble about in the orchard.

"Josh, come here," she called. "I think I see a bear or something up in the orchard."

As Josh stepped up behind her and looked out the window he said, "That's somebody wandering around out there. What crazy fool would be out in this kind of weather?" Just then the figure fell to the ground and lay still.

"I'll get Charlie and we'll go help them to the house," said Josh as he bundled up and headed toward the door. "We'll have to hurry before another storm blows in. Build the fire up and get some quilts ready."

Rebecca watched as they tied rope from trees to posts as they worked their way toward the prone figure. As the storm reached the ranch, visibility diminished, and she lost sight of them. She paced restlessly through the house until she heard them push their way through the door with their burden. They laid him on the table and began working to get the frozen clothes from his body.

"Josh, who is it?" she asked. "Is he alive?"

Josh glanced at Charlie and then came around the table and took her in his arms. "I believe he'll be all right when we get him warmed up. Honey, it's Arthur."

"No…" she cried, struggling to go to him.

"Rebecca," said Josh as give her a gentle shake, "you've got to help us. Fix a pallet in front of the fire, then warm some soup or broth to feed him."

"But why was he out there?" she cried.

"He was trying to knock the ice and snow from the limbs of the fruit trees. It looks like he has been out there for quite a while. The bright sunshine reflecting off the snow blinded him, and he couldn't find his way back to the cabin." Going over to where Rachael held a sobbing Levi, he said, "Take Levi to our bedroom and entertain him until we get things settled in here."

They stripped the cold wet clothes off and wrapped Arthur in warm quilts, laying him by the fire on the pallet. Rebecca sat with his head in her lap. The tears ran down her cheeks as she tried to spoon the broth between the cold, stiff lips. After she managed to get a few spoonfuls down and the fire began to warm his cold body, he started to move.

"Don't cry, Miss Becky, I'll be fine."

Rebecca wrapped her arms around his silvery gray head and rocked gently as the tears flowed.

"My eyes hurt," he mumbled.

"Arthur, it's from snow blindness," said Josh as he took the old man's hand in his. "It will clear up in a couple of days. You just rest."

He slept well into the night, and Rebecca stayed close by. In the early hours of the morning, she awoke to his hoarse, raspy breathing and a fever. His age had prevented his body from fighting off the pneumonia that sometimes occurs after severe exposure to the cold weather. Rebecca woke Josh, and they began applying hot compresses to his chest to ease the pain and try to break the congestion. They battled with the fever all the next day and up into the next night, but he slowly grew weaker.

"Josh, we've got to get a doctor for him," Rebecca pleaded with fear in her eyes.

"There's no way we can get him here, not with this storm still raging," said Josh sadly. "Even if the storm stopped I doubt that anyone could make it to town."

They had moved him to their bedroom where it was quieter, and Rebecca dozed in a chair by Arthur's side. She awoke to hear him mumbling.

"Jesus, I hear you. I'm coming," Arthur whispered weakly. "Oh I see Jesus, Miss Becky."

During his final moments Arthur beamed with such radiance that they knew he saw his savior, and he'd stretched out his arms to embrace him, his great heavenly love. Arthur had gone home.

Josh sat with Rebecca on his lap as she wept with grief. "Why did he have to die, Josh?" she cried. "He was so happy in his little cabin. He … he was looking forward to working for you this summer and he had so many plans to improve the orchard. Why, Josh?"

"I believe God sees death in a different light than man," replied Josh with a thoughtful expression. "To God, death is a beginning, not an ending. Arthur may have been happy in his cabin, but it was just a resting place on his way to his mansion in heaven."

Rebecca sat quietly for a few minutes, then said, "You're right, Josh. We seem to become so selfish when we have to part with a loved one, although we know they are going to a better place, a place free from pain, sorrow, and the trials of this life. But, he did love his little home. I would like to bury him on the little knoll beside his cabin."

It took the men all day to remove the snow and dig the grave in the hard, frozen, stony ground. Arthur was laid to rest later that day. Josh refused to let Rebecca and the children face the bitter cold and take the chance of one of them becoming sick. They watched sadly from the window as their dear friend was lowered into the grave.

Josh could tell that deep inside, Rebecca grieved daily because of the death of her friend Arthur. The winter months allowed her too much time to think of her sorrow. He was glad they had the children to occupy much of her time. With Arthur gone, she had taken over their schooling, and that filled many hours of the winter days.

Chapter Seventeen

> *For the wicked boasteth of his heart's desire, and blesseth the covetous, whom the Lord abhorreth.*
>
> Psalm 10:3

It was a cool spring day in April when George Pickett arrived in Longmont. He looked at the dusty, western town with disdain and wondered why anyone would choose to live in such an uncultured area. He was here for one reason only: to get the uppity Rebecca and take her back east where she belonged, one way or another. He possessed the self-assured attitude that whoever this poor rancher was whom she had married, he would have no trouble convincing him that Rebecca was his wife, and that she had tricked him into marrying her when she already had a husband. Just for security, he had a forged marriage license containing both of their names and dated two years prior. Now all he had to do was look around town and find a couple of men who would do anything for a little money. He always had a way of locating these characters.

A little cash was all it had taken to get the boy at the post office back home to watch for a letter to the Rileys from Rebecca. When he was shown the letter, he had taken note of the name of the town and, recognizing her handwriting, he had all the information he needed. He had just sat tight until spring weather arrived to start his detrimental trip west.

He sauntered over to one of the cheaper-looking saloons where he was more likely to find the kind of man needed for the job he had in mind. An hour later his wait was rewarded when he heard a half-drunken bloke quarreling about a Mr. Holt who had stolen his cook. Soon he was on a barstool next to a man called Hank, buying him drinks, when the name Holt was brought up again.

"What did this Holt guy do to you, Hank?" George asked innocently.

"He 'tole my girl," Hank stammered, trying to get the words to come out right. "Just load 'er in 'is wagon and rode off 'ith 'er. Him and his wife, Rebecca."

"What was this fellow's first name?" he asked, pouring Hank another shot of whiskey.

"Joshua, Joshua Holt," he answered with a sneer.

"Hank, old man, I know just how you feel," he said, placing an arm reluctantly around the dusty shoulders. "He took my woman, too," George said, thinking that Hank was referring to a girlfriend.

"He did?" said the shocked drunk, looking with disbelief at George.

"Yes," he said with an exaggerated sigh. "That Rebecca is my wife who ran off last spring, and I have just now tracked her down. Don't let anyone know, but I've come to take her home, and I don't want it to get around about what kind of woman she is."

"Can ya believe that," said the suddenly sobered Hank. "Them religious ones are the ones you have to watch, don't ya."

"Yes, she always did put on a pious act in front of people, but with that red hair, she is a pure hellcat. I'll probably have to hire a couple of fellows to help me just so she won't cause a scene. You know of any fellows looking for a little cash who can keep their mouths shut?" he inquired innocently.

"Why, it'd be my pleasure to help, and I know just the fellow we can get to help us. He could use a little money right now." Hank had had Snake watching the ranch, hoping to get even with Josh for protecting Rachael and her small brother.

"You get in touch with him and meet me here tonight after supper. Just be sure to keep your mouth shut so she won't get the word I'm in town and give me the slip again."

With satisfaction, he checked into a hotel and after changing clothes, went down to supper. When he returned to the saloon, he saw the two men waiting for him. With a satisfied smile at their unscrupulous appearance, he walked over, sat down, and ordered the bartender to bring a round of whiskey.

"Mr. Pickett," Hank said in a half whisper, "I

been thinking, and it's not going to be so easy to get your wife away from that Josh Holt. He thinks the world of her. He will probably do everything he can to get her back."

"Not when I show him the marriage license," George said with a gloating expression.

"But she's going to have his kid! A man won't give up his kid as easy as a no account woman," he replied, not seeing the shocked expression that George let slip.

This was something George hadn't counted on, but he wasn't stopping now. He would get rid of the kid later. He sure wasn't going to raise another man's child.

"You got any ideas how I should go about getting her back east without trouble?" he asked.

"You goin' back by train?' Hank inquired.

"Yes," he answered, "I've got two return tickets in my pocket."

"Snake, here," he said, nodding toward the shifty looking partner, "says that Holt and his men are building a fence a ways up from the house. It would be best if you take your wife while he's not home. That way you can get a head start. Instead of leaving from Longmont, I'd flag the train down at the watering station about fifteen miles from the ranch house and take it to Fort Collins. He'd never think about you going north."

George thought this plan over and even though he didn't think any man would chase down a woman who had lied to him, he would follow this plan because he felt these men were more familiar with the territory than he was. Even if Holt did catch up with him later, no man would want Rebecca after he got through with her, he thought with a sneer. He counted himself lucky to have run across someone who already held a grudge against Holt.

They planned to meet outside of town about noon. Snake had informed them that the young girl who stayed with them always rode out with the men's lunch and was gone several hours, and the kid was always playing outside and wouldn't be a problem.

The next day as they topped the ridge looking down on the ranch, George was surprised at the prosperous looking spread and thought that his Rebecca had settled herself well. Little good it would do her now, though. He rode in a hired, closed carriage, and the men led on horseback. They had watched from cover as the girl headed out, riding toward where the men were building a fence.

Hank had spotted the boy up behind the house playing in the creek and knew that he wouldn't notice their arrival. As they pulled up to the house, Rebecca wondered who would be visiting in a buggy at this time of day. She went into the kitchen to take off her apron and was smoothing her hair when there was a knock at the door.

She opened the door and quickly stepped back, gasping with shock at the sight of her dreaded enemy standing there with a smirk of satisfaction on his face.

"Well, well, Rebecca, dear," he sneered, "aren't you going to invite me in?"

"George!" she said with fear in her eyes, "What are you doing here?"

"I've come to get my wife," he said, pushing his way through the doorway.

"But, I told you I couldn't marry you. Didn't you get my letter?" she asked, trying to control her old fear of this man.

"Oh, yes," he answered, "I got the note, lying about you having a position to go to."

"Well, I did. I got married, so you're too late!" she snapped, getting her spunk back.

"So I noticed," he said with another sneer, eyeing her slightly swollen stomach with repulsion. Even in her condition, though, she looked better than ever. "But that man you supposedly married won't have a thing to do with you when he sees our marriage license and knows how you tricked him."

"Marriage license? What are you talking about?" she asked, feeling that this couldn't be happening. *Oh, God help me,* she prayed silently.

He pulled a legal-looking paper from his pocket, holding it up for her to see, but keeping it out of her reach. She gasped as she read their names on the document and made a grab for it as he laughed and said, "I don't think so, my dear. We will just leave this here on the table, and he will understand," he finished, motioning for the other men to come in.

When Hank appeared at the door with an evil grin, she turned and ran toward the back door but was caught roughly just as she reached for the handle. She screamed and kicked out at anyone who tried to help subdue her until Hank said in her ear with a snarl, "Remember, you're in a delicate condition."

Sobbing, she was half-dragged and half-carried to the carriage where George waited with a look of satisfaction and roughly pushed her inside. The carriage pulled away from the house, carrying in it Josh's most cherished love.

Chapter Eighteen

> *The Lord also will be a refuge for the oppressed, a refuge in time of trouble. And they that know thy name will put their trust in thee: for thou, Lord, hast not forsaken them that seek thee.*
>
> Psalm 9:9–10

Rachael was enjoying the ride in the warm spring air. Josh had taught her to ride on the fair days during the winter, and she could now be trusted on her own. She had ridden about a mile when she realized she had left one of the baskets of sandwiches in the barn when she had saddled Pepper. Turning, she urged the mare, which was ready for a good outing, to head back toward the barn. When she came in sight of the house she saw the carriage and two men on horseback. She stopped in a stand of trees to see if she knew them. Easing forward in the saddle, she gasped when she recognized her old enemy, Hank. Not wishing to be spotted, she hung close to the buildings as she worked her way to the barn. She tied Pepper to a hitch and sneaked in the side door and up to the loft for a closer look. As she peeked through a crack, she stifled a scream of terror as she saw Hank and another man drag Rebecca out to the carriage and push her inside. She stared in disbelief as the carriage pulled out with the two riders leading the way.

With tears streaming down her face, Rachael hung on to the horse as she raced to where Josh and the men were working. Josh saw her riding at such a dangerous pace and feared the horse was out of control. He jumped on Duchess and rode out to meet her. Seeing him approach, she jumped from the saddle and flung herself into his arms, crying out of control.

"Rachael, what's wrong?" he asked, trying to pry her trembling hands from his neck. "Has Levi been hurt?"

"No! They... they got Miss Becky," she stammered, trying to control her tears. "They pushed her into a carriage and took her away."

"Rachael," he cried, giving her a slight shake, "what are you talking about!" Tremors of fear ran down his spine like lightening.

"Hank and another man dragged Miss Becky out of the house, pushed her into a black carriage, and took her away," she repeated with a new rush of tears.

With another bolt of fear rushing through his body for her safety, he rode up to the men and yelled. "Take care of Rachael and get back to the ranch. Brent and Charlie, come with me. Something has happened to Rebecca. Which way did they go?" he asked the sobbing girl, as the men mounted their horses.

"Toward town, I think," she answered.

Josh and the men rode over the hills, hoping to cut them off before they reached town, not realizing they had turned to the north as soon as they were out of sight of the house. With the road so heavily traveled, Josh could not tell he was going the opposite direction, away from Rebecca and her captors.

The lathered horses came to a stop in front of the sheriff's office and Josh dismounted, running through the door. Sheriff Callahan, who was half-asleep with his feet propped upon his desk, jumped up with a start.

"They kidnapped Rebecca!" Josh cried to a startled Callahan, "Hank and a man in a black carriage just dragged her from the house and drove away!"

"What!" exclaimed the sheriff; "I just saw Hank and a man called Snake in town this morning. They were seen drinking with a stranger at The Blue Goose last night. Why would they take your wife?"

"I don't know," he replied, with a vengeance in his voice. "But just wait 'til I get my hands on them. They better not hurt a hair on her head."

Soon they were headed back toward the ranch with a group of armed men, looking for clues to where the carriage had turned off. Just two miles from the ranch, they saw the carriage tracks turn off on a seldom-used wagon road.

"That leads to the water tank," said one of the men. "I bet they've flagged down the train."

In a cloud of dust, the men raced down the road at a breakneck speed, hoping to reach the tracks before the train finished filling up with water.

"Oh God, let us be in time," Josh prayed, realizing he hadn't slowed down long enough to pray. His mind was in turmoil, trying to come up with a reason for someone to have a desire to hurt Rebecca, who had never hurt anyone.

An hour later as they topped the hill that led down to the tracks, the sheriff quickly motioned them back. The train had already left, and a black carriage was coming up the road with two horses tied behind. The men quietly moved into the shadow of the trees on either side of the road, and waited.

Hank and Snake leisurely rode up the road, headed back to town to spend their money. The evening shadows were just invading the roadway when they passed the group of trees. The posse rushed out, surrounded the carriage, and pointed their guns at the startled occupants.

"Ok, fellows, let's hand those weapons over real easy like and step down," said the sheriff. "What are you doing riding around in the country in a fancy buggy and it almost night?"

Hank, quick to recover, said with a laugh, "Why we just took one of my friends from back east to catch the train."

"Why couldn't he just get on in town?" questioned Callahan, suspiciously.

"He had some business out this way and didn't want to wait 'til tomorrow to start back, so he just had us drive him over here to flag down the north-bound," said Hank, feeling self-confident. "Who you lookin' for, Callahan?" he said innocently.

"We're looking for my wife," said Josh, stepping out of the shadows, not able to contain himself any longer. Grabbing Hank roughly by the front of his shirt, he asked him, "Where is she? If she's hurt in any way, you'll pay dearly."

"I don't know what you're talking about," said Hank with a sneer.

"Take it easy, Josh," interrupted the sheriff, "you'd better let me handle this." Turning to Hank, he asked, "Who was this friend of yours?"

"Why, George Pickett. He came out looking for his wife that ran away last spring. He heard she was living in adultery with someone by the name of Holt, so I just showed him where she was," he answered, looking at Josh with a gleam of triumph.

"Why, you ... " started Josh, but Charlie pulled him back, putting his arm around his boss.

"Don't pay him no mind, and you know it's not true. Bet she's back at the house with supper on the table, waiting on you."

"No," said Josh, sadly, "not with Pickett mixed up in it. He's an old enemy of Rebecca's, and I fear for her safety."

"Hank, you and Snake are under arrest for aiding in the kidnapping of Rebecca Holt. Tie them up, men," said Callahan.

"Now, wait just a minute, Sheriff," said Hank. "It ain't against the law for a man to take his wife home.

He showed me the marriage license and left it on Holt's table so he'd know where she went."

"How do you know what it said?" mocked Callahan, "You can't read. Take them to town and lock 'em up," he said to his deputy. "Then send a wire immediately to the sheriff in Fort Collins. Tell him to meet the train and arrest Mr. Pickett and put Mrs. Holt up in a hotel. Tell him I'll be there tomorrow. Come on, Son," he said to the dejected Josh, "let's ride back to your house and have a look around."

The marriage license was on the table where George had left it. As Josh stood looking at the paper, Rachael came running from her room.

"Did you find Miss Becky?" she cried. Looking past the silent Josh, the sheriff shook his head. "Oh, Mr. Josh, you got to look harder," she pleaded. But Josh just walked to his room and closed the door.

The sheriff walked over and said, "Don't worry, Missy, we know who has her and where they are headed. It's just a matter of time before she is home again."

In the bedroom, Josh sat on the edge of the bed with his head in his hands. *Lord, I just can't believe this is real. She has been my faithful and loving wife these past months and I have never caught her in a lie. Lord, I feel in my heart that this is just a scheme of her old enemy, to get revenge. Just protect her, Lord, send a guardian angel to be by her side, to show her what she must do to stay safe. Show me the way to reach her quickly and bring her home safe. Amen.*

Chapter Nineteen

The eyes of the Lord are in every place, beholding the evil and the good.

Proverbs 15: 3

The locomotive blasted a throaty warning, emitting a cloud of steam as the cars jerked into motion along the track. As the train rumbled out of sight of the watering station, George sat watching the slight sway of her body, as Rebecca lay in the sleeping berth, oblivious to what was going on about her. Things were going better than he had hoped. As soon as Hank had pushed her into the carriage he had slipped a chloroform- soaked cloth over her mouth and nose, rendering her unconscious. When they arrived at the watering station, he sought out the conductor and told him his wife was sick and that he must get her to a doctor in Fort Collins. He demanded a section in the sleeping car. The conductor gave no thought to the situation as George carried her, unconscious, to his assigned berth.

They had traveled for a while when she began to

moan and stir, trying to fight her way back to consciousness. The train had just stopped at a small station, and a passenger was coming into the car just as she realized her situation.

"Where are you taking me?" she shouted, trying to get out of the curtained section, "Josh will kill you when he finds me."

"Shut up, Rebecca!" he hissed, through clenched teeth, glancing skittishly at the newcomer who was busy putting his belongings in the section across the aisle.

She started to fight and kick, knocked the curtain aside, and exposed her frightened face to the man just before the drugged cloth was slipped once again over her face, and the curtain pulled back in place.

———◆———

Just outside of Loveland at a small depot, a weary Jonathan Smith boarded the train, heading toward Fort Collins, where he was to hold a meeting. As he walked into the sleeping section, he heard a woman shout from behind a curtain across the aisle, "Where are you taking me? Josh will kill you when he finds me." He glanced over as the woman began to kick at the curtain, and he beheld the terror-filled face of Rebecca Holt. A hand slipped a white cloth over her face, then pulled the curtain closed.

Puzzled, but pretending to show no interest in the situation, he stowed his belongings and discreetly walked to the next car and searched out the conductor.

"Who is supposed to be in the berth across the aisle from me?" he asked impatiently.

"Why, Mr. Pickett, Sir. His wife is sick and he's taking her to Fort Collins to a doctor. Is something wrong?" asked the conductor.

"There sure is! That is not his wife!" he exclaimed, "That is Rebecca Holt, wife of Joshua Holt who lives outside of Longmont."

"Surely you're mistaken," he replied. "The man said—"

"I don't care what the man said! I am the pastor of Shadow Valley Baptist Church, and Rebecca Holt and her husband are members there, and I see them every Sunday. Something is going on, and I don't like the looks of it. I saw him put something over her face when she started fighting him, then everything got quiet in their berth."

"I'll go check and see ..." said the man.

"No, we mustn't make him suspicious," cautioned Jonathan. "Can you send a wire anywhere before we reach Fort Collins?"

"Yes," he replied, "Loveland is just ahead."

"Get off and send a wire to the sheriff in Fort Collins," Jonathan instructed the man. "Tell him to meet the train and we will turn the situation over to him, but we must keep a watch and be sure nothing happens to her. I believe she is expecting a child."

Jonathan returned to his section and climbed in. He lay tensely, listening to every sound from across the aisle. *What in the world could be going on?* There could be no mistake at the terror on her face or the warning in the man's voice as he had shut her up. He could do nothing now except pray. He bowed his head, entreating the Lord to protect this dear young woman and to enable him to help her out of this frightening situation.

When the train arrived in Fort Collins, Jonathan watched as the man picked up the unconscious Rebecca, struggling to make it to the platform with his burden.

"Can I help you, Sir?" he offered.

"No, thanks," he replied with a look of suspicion, "I can manage."

"I am a preacher if you should need anything. Is the woman sick?" he asked innocently.

"Yes, I must get her to a doctor, immediately," the man said, stepping to the platform.

The conductor stood on the steps and caught the eye of the sheriff, indicating the suspect. The sheriff stepped up and asked, "Sir can I help? Is the lady sick?"

"Yes!" shouted the man. He wondered from where so many Good Samaritans appeared. "And no, I don't need help."

"Take her over to the hotel and put her in a room," the sheriff suggested, "then you can get a doctor."

As he crossed the street, not being a person accustomed to strenuous work, he struggled to step up on the sidewalk, the veins in his neck protruding with the strain.

"Please, let me help you," pleaded Jonathan, who

had not let them out of his sight. The man reluctantly gave up his burden.

As Jonathan laid Rebecca on the bed in the hotel room, the sheriff turned to the man and said, "You said your name was George Pickett?"

"Yes," he replied, then realized he had not given his name.

"You're under arrest for the kidnapping of Mrs. Joshua Holt," said the sheriff, pulling a pair of handcuffs from his belt.

"You don't know what you are talking about," sneered George, starting to feel a little nervous about the turnaround in the situation. "That lady is my wife!"

"That's not what the sheriff in Longmont wired me earlier. So you can just spend the night with me until I get to the bottom of this," he replied. He placed the cuffs on George and then led him away.

Just then, Rebecca started to come around again. Opening her eyes, still full of terror, she saw Brother Smith sitting in a chair by her bed gently holding her hand.

"Brother Smith, how did you get here?" she asked, disoriented, "Where's Josh! Oh, no ... "

"It's all right," he said, trying to calm her. "How come you were on the train with this George fellow?" he asked as a man came into the room carrying a medical bag.

"Oh," she moaned again, tears filling her eyes, "He came to the ranch insisting that he was my husband and that he had a license to prove it. It's a lie!

He is an old enemy from back east. He had Hank with him, and they grabbed me and shoved me into a buggy. That's all I remember except waking up and feeling like I was on a train."

"It's okay, Rebecca. Mr. Pickett is in jail, under arrest for kidnapping," he said, patting her hand. "He must have drugged you, so a doctor is here to check on you. Just rest and I'll go send Josh a wire and let him know you are safe."

The effect of being drugged had left her groggy, and she slept until afternoon, awakening to discover Josh sitting on the edge of the bed, tears streaming down his face, worried about her condition but happy to see her safely out of George's clutches.

She threw herself into his arms, weeping as she told him of her terror.

"I was so afraid I would never see you again. You didn't believe the terrible lies he told, did you?" she asked.

"Not for a minute," he whispered, his face buried in her hair.

"And he's in jail?" she asked.

"Well, he was," he replied, pushing her hair out of her tearstained face, "but he tricked the young deputy into getting too close, knocked him on the head, took the keys, and let himself out. But don't you worry, they are hot on his trail, and will soon catch him."

Josh went to answer a knock at the door and let in a girl to fill a bathtub. While she bathed, he hurried down to the store and came back with new underclothes and a pretty green dress. As she slipped it on, she laughed at the snug fit around the waist.

"You forgot you have a fat wife," she smiled.

"I just knew I never wanted you to wear that dress again, the one you wore when that louse took you," he replied. He gathered up the old clothes and threw them out the back window.

Later, as they sat in the lobby waiting for Sheriff Callahan, the events of the last couple of days caused her to ponder. *The Lord is so good to have let me come out of this without getting hurt or hurting the child I am carrying.* She didn't realize the many prayers that had been issued on her behalf by all her loved ones.

Chapter Twenty

Oh let the wickedness of the wicked come to an end;

Psalm 7:9a

His mischief shall return upon his own head, and his violent dealing shall come down upon his own pate.

Psalm 7:16

George lurked in the shadow of the building and observed the man as he dismounted and went in the back entrance of the saloon. He assumed the man would be occupied for a while, and he quietly untied the horse and led him into the shadows, where he mounted and headed out of town unobserved. His escape from jail had been accomplished in a matter of hours after being escorted there by the sheriff. He snickered to himself as he thought of how gullible the young deputy had been and the ease of his escape. Now he only had to get out of town a ways and once again flag down a train, this time headed east.

As he had sat in the jail earlier, he had decided that another tactic would have to be devised to conquer Rebecca, who had once again escaped his grasp. He would return home and concoct another scheme, this one more devious than the last.

He rode down the road he assumed would lead toward the tracks. It was a dark, cloudy night, and he was unaware of the wrong turns he made, which led him in the opposite direction of his goal. He skirted around the farmhouses with their barking, snarling dogs. He held to the shadowy woods for a distance before he once again entered the road.

He was not a person who enjoyed the outdoors and clung to the comfort that the larger towns provided for conveyance. Neither was he a skilled horseman, and his mount was quick to determine that and use it to its own advantage. The buckskin had not been watered for a while, and sensing water nearby, was determined to reach it, no matter how George tried to maneuver him around the rough outcrop of rocks.

George found himself perched on the edge of a steep ravine, astride a mount bent on reaching the water cascading over the rocks far below. He managed to guide him back onto the path and paused to wipe the webs from his face and adjust his composure. Suddenly, a hair-raising scream came from the huge pine he had just passed beneath and shattered any inkling of bravery he possessed. In one graceful bound, a mountain lion leaped on the haunches of his mount and sent them all down into the deep chasm.

The sun gave forth its weak spring rays, trying to dispel the chill from the air, as the sheriff and a posse headed out of town, following the undisguised trail of their escapee. Sheriff Callahan, accompanied by Joshua Holt, had arrived earlier from Longmont, and Sheriff Long was determined to capture the scoundrel to send back with Callahan. The erratic trail puzzled the pursuers and led them toward the Owl Canyon, an area even experienced horsemen shunned. They soon reached the conclusion that they were following the wandering trail of a confused man. The tracker lost the trail many times in the rocks and gullies, and the sun was high in the sky when they reached the ravine where George had met his end. Below, in a tangle, lay the puma and his prey under the twisted body of the buckskin.

It was late afternoon before they maneuvered their way down the treacherous hillside to recover the body and climb to safety. The tired, dusty group rode into town, the body tied on the back of the sheriff's mount. Callahan, who was filled in on the details, met them.

"We had another victim of an accident from your area back in the fall," reported the sheriff. "Man by the name of John Smith was found up at an old mine site, half buried by a rock slide. The man who found him said Smith was alive and gave him his name and where he lived. Said he had two kids he had to get home to, but he never survived the trip down the mountain."

"Yes, I know the kids," Callahan said sadly. "They gave up hope of their pa coming home, and they now live with the Holts."

He slowly walked over to the hotel to report to Josh. He found Josh and Rebecca waiting in the lobby. She was rested and looked refreshed in a new dress, impatiently waiting to head for home. He had meant to give the news to Josh first, but she met him and asked, "Did they find him? Can we go home now?"

"Yes, he was found, Ma'am, but he met a terrible death." He cast a worried look at Josh.

"What happened?" asked Josh, as he slipped an arm around Rebecca's waist.

"He met up with one of our local puma and ended up at the bottom of a ravine with his horse on top of him."

"Oh, no! He's dead?" asked the shocked Rebecca.

"Yes, Mrs. Holt, but it's no more than he deserves, after the way he treated you."

"But, he was not saved," she replied in anguish. "I tried so many times to tell him about the Lord, but he would just laugh it off."

"Honey, you did your duty," comforted Josh, "and the Lord is the only one who could have saved him."

"I know, but it's so sad. Even though I was terrified of him, I don't want anyone to die and go to hell."

"Do you know his family and who to notify of his death?" inquired the sheriff.

"He didn't have any family that I know of. He was a business partner to my uncle who passed away last summer. When he died, he stated in his will that I was to marry George if I was to receive half of his estate. You know," she said, with a confused look on her face, "I seem to remember George bragging about me not being intelligent enough to read the will for myself, when we were on the train."

"Josh, I think you'd better hire a good lawyer to check that out. Wire your brother to get a lawyer started on it before he heads out here with his family. I have some more bad news to tell you. The sheriff here told me the pa of those Smith kids you've been keeping was killed last fall in a rock slide."

"Oh, Josh, that means we can keep them!" she beamed, then quickly added, "I mean, I'm sorry he died, but he was not much of a father to the children."

"That's true, Ma'am, but they are officially orphans now and will have to be turned over to the state."

"You mean we can't keep them? But they have a home. Why would they have to go to an orphanage?" cried an anguished Rebecca. She turned to Josh, hoping for some reassurance.

"Ma'am, that will be up to the adoption board. But you might get a lawyer for that too, to speed it up."

"We'll talk it over, Sheriff, but right now I want

to get my wife home. By the time we get a bite to eat and head to the station, it should be time for the train."

They talked and prayed over the different situations facing them and came to the conclusion that Sheriff Callahan was right. They needed a lawyer to check into the legal procedures for adopting the Smith children as soon as possible. Rebecca didn't want them to have to spend one night away from the ranch in the care of strangers.

The question about the will was to be wired to Matt requesting him to hire a lawyer to look into it. They decided they weren't interested in the financial gain, but needed to get it settled and off their minds. When they arrived in Longmont early the next morning, they saw a lawyer who had advised Josh on other matters, then sent a wire off to Matt.

A tired couple rode toward home with a thankful heart and rejoiced that God had delivered Rebecca to safety.

Chapter Twenty-One

Trust in the Lord with all thine heart; and lean not unto thine own understanding. In all thy ways acknowledge him, and he shall direct thy paths.

Proverbs 3:5–6

They approached the ranch and saw Rachael pacing on the front porch. As she caught sight of the wagon, she ran down the road, her joy at the sight of her Miss Becky giving wings to her feet. As she drew near, Josh stopped, and she climbed into the wagon. She wept as she was gathered into Rebecca's comforting arms.

"Oh, Miss Becky, I was so scared," she cried. "I saw 'em push you in the carriage an' I just knew you were dead."

"I'm not hurt, Rachael, honey," she said, stroking the silky black curls. "I'm home now and we don't have to worry about that happening again." She told her what had happened to George. Taking Rachael's face gently between her hands, she also told her of her father's death. Rachael sat back on the wagon seat and held on to Rebecca's hand, but never spoke a word.

Josh started the team on down toward the house where most of the men were waiting to welcome the missus home. She spotted Levi as he ran across the field, his black and white puppy bounding at his heels.

Josh gently lifted Rebecca down from the wagon and followed her inside. "Honey, I want you go straight to bed and lie down for the rest of the day."

"But, Josh, I have so much to do," she exclaimed, looking around the room.

"I don't see a thing that needs to be done," he remarked, noting the neat appearance of the house. "Looks like our Rachael has everything under control."

Rachael stood timidly in the doorway. "I done everything just like you taught me, Miss Becky," she said. "I just have one more load of clothes to hang out and then I hav'ta bake the bread that's risin'. You best do what Mr. Josh says."

With a smile at the concern on her loved ones' faces, she said, "I am kind of tired, so I'll rest until it's time to prepare supper, if it will make you two happy." She went to her room and removed her new dress, then put on a blue dressing gown and stretched out on the bed. She had been concerned about not feeling the baby move very much the last couple of days but, as she relaxed, it renewed its activity knowing it was safe at home. She was almost in her seventh month, and not having been around women in this condition, was not aware that her size was anything but normal. She had only one dress that she could wear, and Josh had thrown it away. She had to sew herself a couple of dresses even if she wouldn't be wearing them long.

Outside her window an energetic brown wren had built its nest in the clematis vine that climbed up the lattice. Its mate serenaded her from the branches of a cherry tree. A warm spring breeze, heavily perfumed with honeysuckle, gently lifted the ruffled curtains. Rebecca watched out the window as Brad worked on a picket fence that Josh was having him build around the yard. The meadow was covered with wildflowers, and it joined the rambling brook as it gurgled over the boulders on its way to the lower valley. In the distance the mountains were still snow-capped. This was a beautiful land, and she had learned to love it just as she had learned to love her husband.

She tried to sleep, but the episode of the last few days crowded into her mind, replaying the events in detail. She thanked God that he had willed for Jonathan Smith to be on that train and to come to her rescue. Even though she had been filled with terror, God had had control of the situation, and it had worked out for her good. She would never have to worry about George again, even though she was grieved by his death. They had also learned the fate of the children's father, and she and Josh now felt that they were free to call Rachael and Levi their own.

Finally, sleep overcame her active mind. She awoke later to the aroma of freshly baked bread drifting from the kitchen. She was so glad she had Rachael to help her this spring. Matthew and Hannah would arrive with their children in a few weeks, and they would stay with them until their house was built. She would have Rachael help her tomorrow, and they would start on the bedrooms upstairs and get them ready for Matthew's family. Josh had told her they had a daughter, Drucilla, who was the same age as Rachael, and Rebecca hoped she would be good company for her. Their son Martin was eight, and the baby, Melinda, was five.

Rebecca put on the green dress Josh had bought her yesterday, leaving the buttons undone at the waist. She put on a big white apron and then headed to the kitchen. Rachael was at the table peeling potatoes for supper. Rebecca bent over and gave her a kiss on her rosy cheek and said, "I want to thank you for the wonderful job you did while I was away."

"Oh, Miss Becky, I was so worried I couldn't sleep or even sit still so I jus' worked. I got the little gown finished for the baby that you cut out for me. It's so little! I can't believe Levi was ever that small."

"They sure grow up fast. This one I carry now seems to need more room every day. I want us to start on the rooms upstairs while I can still fit in the stairway," Rebecca said with a laugh.

She mixed up some cornbread and put it in the oven to go with the dried beans Rachael had cooked. As she sliced the potatoes to fry, she noticed that

Rachael had become quiet. She went ahead and set the table while Rachael took out the peelings and fed them to the chickens.

When she came back in she looked at Rebecca and said, "How come I can't cry about Pa? I loved Pa, but I can't believe that he's really dead."

"Maybe it's because your father was away from home so much. It just doesn't seem real to you yet, but I know you loved him. I knew my mother was dying, and I thought I was prepared, but it was weeks after she was gone before I really started missing her. I would be working on something and think, 'I'll ask Mother if this is right,' then I would realize that she was gone. It took God's grace to get me through that time of grief. Even though I knew she was in heaven, free from pain and suffering, I still felt like I had been abandoned. But my faith in God helped me through, helped me accept that she was gone, and gave me assurance that I would see her again in heaven. You have the same God to call upon now that you have accepted Christ into your life. Just tell him all your doubts and fears, and he will give you the comfort you need."

"I will," Rachael said with teary eyes. "I'm so glad you and Mr. Josh have shown me how to trust in God. Ma always loved God, and I know he helped her through the rough years she had with Pa. I just wish Pa had been saved, too."

"I'm sure your father had heard the Gospel since your mother was a Bible reading woman. We don't know what went through his mind as he lay pinned under those rocks. That may have been the only way God could get his attention and cause him to realize his need of him. You may not know until you reach heaven, but whatever happened was God's will, and we must accept it."

"Ma did talk to Pa about God, and sometimes he would listen to her. He always got a real sad look on his face like he wished he could have her faith in God."

Hearing a rider approach, Rachael went to the door and looked out. "It's Sheriff Callahan," she said, turning to Rebecca. "I wonder what he wants?"

Rebecca stepped out on the porch as he dismounted and came up the new flagstone walk Brad had just built.

"Good afternoon, Mrs. Holt," he greeted. He removed his dusty hat that covered his sparse, graying hair. "Looks like you are recovering from your encounter."

"I'm fine, Mr. Callahan. Won't you come in? Josh should be here soon."

"I'll just sit here on this porch swing. It's looks real inviting," he said, as he sat down and stretched out his long legs.

"Rachael, bring the sheriff a glass of apple cider," she called into the house.

"That sounds delicious, Ma'am" he said, as Rachael carried out a frosty glass of the refreshing drink. "Ma'am, I just came out to inform you I would be out to pick up the children in the morning. They have to go to Denver to the orphanage since we know their father is dead."

"No!" cried Rebecca. She cast a concerned look toward the bewildered Rachael. "I will not let them be taken away from us. We have a lawyer working on the adoption papers now."

"I'm real sorry Ma'am, but I have my orders to put them on the train in the morning. When you get the papers from your lawyer, I'm sure you can go get the children."

"If they have to go to Denver then I'm going with them and you can bet they will be coming right back home with me," replied Rebecca angrily.

"Ma'am, I hope you are right, but are you sure you're up to another train ride in your condition?" he asked with concern.

"If that's what it takes to keep the children with me, then I am sure God will give me the strength to make the trip," she replied with confidence.

"Well, Ma'am, if that's what you want, I'll just meet you in town early in the morning. Good day," he said, as he walked out and mounted his horse and headed back toward town.

She turned to find Rachael with tears streaming down her cheeks. "Are you and Mr. Josh really going to adopt us?" she asked, smiling through her tears.

"That's what we want if it's all right with you and Levi. We just hadn't had time to sit down and talk it over with you. The sheriff said we might have to get a lawyer, so we stopped this morning when we got to town and saw Mr. Jamison."

"Oh, Miss Becky, I'll be a real good daughter to you and I know Levi will be so happy. He ain't ever had a real mother."

"Well, I'm just sorry we have to go to Denver, but don't you worry. I won't return home until I can bring you both back with me."

They stood in the kitchen wrapped in each other's arms when Josh came in the door with Levi on his back, the pup bounding right at their heels. "What's wrong?" he asked when he saw the tears. "Who was that rider?"

Rebecca told him what had taken place while Rachael took Levi to get washed up for supper. Josh was concerned about the trip she was determined to take with the children, and decided to ride in after supper and talk to Mr. Jamison and see if there was any way out of it. If they had to make the trip, he was going, too. Everyone was quiet during supper except Levi. They had decided not to tell him about the orphanage, just that they were taking a train ride in the morning.

Rebecca packed some clothes for the trip. She neatly inserted some strips of material under the arms of two of her cotton dresses, giving her some much needed room. The new material was brighter than the dresses, since they had been washed many times and were slightly faded. She was glad it was still cool enough that she could wear the fringed shawl her Uncle Hess had given her one Christmas. It would hide the alterations.

Josh came in late that night from seeing the lawyer. He had the adoption papers ready to be signed by the adoption board, but he had been informed that they would still have to take the children to Denver.

As he held Rebecca in his arms that night, they prayed together that God would be with them on their trip. They were assured it was God's will for the children to be with them, so they would face tomorrow with confidence.

Chapter Twenty-Two

As arrows are in the hand of a mighty man; so are children of the youth. Happy is the man that hath his quiver full of them...

Psalm 127:4–5a

Rebecca packed a lunch to take on the train and sent it out to the wagon with Rachael while she herself checked to see if everything was in order in the house.

When Rachael put the basket in the back of the wagon, Brent approached, and she gave him a timid smile.

Brent took her small hand in his, laying in her palm a tiny bird point arrowhead made of black obsidian. "Take this with you to remember me by until you come home again. I'll miss you, Rachael," he said, and then hurried away as he saw Josh come out of the house with the baggage.

Rachael quickly climbed into the back of the wagon. Her heart fluttered in her bosom as she watched Brent mount his appaloosa and turn to wave before he headed out on the range. She clutched the arrowhead in her hand until he was out of sight and then placed it in her pocket, a smile on her face.

They arrived at the station and found the sheriff waiting for them. Josh unloaded their baggage onto the platform and then hurried toward the livery stable to leave the team and wagon. Rebecca walked into the dim station, and memories flooded her mind. She recalled the last time she had been inside, waiting in vain for Josh to appear to claim his bride. With a smile she walked over to the clerk and purchased their tickets.

As the train pulled away from the station, Levi became so excited, jumping and bouncing about, that Rebecca threatened to tie him to the seat. Josh intervened and got him interested in the many sights they passed.

It had been dark the last time Rebecca had traveled from Denver, so this time she watched the changing landscape with wonder. Farmers tilled their fields and planted crops. Herds of cattle grazed on the tender, spring grass. As the train crossed slowly over streams, Rebecca gazed into the limpid water and could see rainbow trout swim lazily about. A majestic eagle soared high in the sky, guarding its domain as it searched for prey to take to its fledglings nestled high on a cliff. On the open range she observed a herd of buffalo, greatly diminished from the mighty herds that once roamed these valleys.

When they arrived in Denver, Rebecca smiled as

the children watched with amazement the bustling crowd on the streets. They checked in at the same hotel she and Arthur had stayed in last summer. It seemed ages ago.

They wanted to get the worrisome ordeal behind them, so they headed straight to the orphanage, but left Rachael to watch over Levi in their room. They followed the directions the clerk at the hotel gave them. They had been informed that a Miss McCleese was in charge. As they approached the orphanage, they were appalled at the condition of the building that housed the orphans. The gray, weathered, three-story building was in dire need of repair. There were many broken windowpanes that let in the cold and rain. There were no children outside, but when Josh opened the front door they saw a room to their left where a class of small children was doing lessons while a stern-faced teacher ambled among the desks. A girl of about thirteen scrubbed the stairway. Two younger girls, down on their knees, were scrubbing the lobby floor. A woman with stringy, graying hair in a dingy dress stood at the top of the stairs and watched the girls work. She hurried down the stairs when she saw the Holts walk in.

"May I help you?" she asked in a cold voice.

"Yes. My name is Joshua Holt, and this is my wife Rebecca. We are here to see Miss McCleese about some children we brought from Longmont," replied Josh.

"That must be the Smith children I heard her talking about. I sure will be glad to get a girl that's old enough to do some of the work. Seems as soon as they reach the age to be of some help, they run off and get married or somthin'. Miss McCleese is busy right now, but I'll let her know you're here. Where's the children?" she asked, glancing out the door to see if they were outside.

"The children are not staying here, so we left them at the hotel," said Rebecca, trying to keep her temper in check. "We are going to adopt them ourselves and have come only to get the papers signed."

"Well, I don't know about that," the woman replied in a nasal-toned voice. "It takes a long time to get that all worked out, so you might as well get the kids since Miss McCleese is busy. I need the girl to help clean out the barn stalls. We don't have no boys to do the heavy work. People keep coming to get them to work on their farms."

"We'll just wait," said Josh quickly. He saw that Rebecca was about to lose her temper at the woman's words.

"I can't let you in her office, so you'll just have to wait here." She hurried down the hall to the back of the house, warning the girls not to shirk while she was gone if they didn't want a strappin'.

They waited quite a while and when no one appeared, Josh asked the young girl who was cleaning the stairs if she knew where the mistress was. She glanced around nervously, and then said, "She's down in the cellar punishing little Jimmy."

"What do you mean by punishing?" asked Rebecca. "What did he do?"

"He didn't do nothin'!" she exclaimed with anger in her eyes. "He just saved a piece of bread from supper last night. She caught him eating it and accused him of stealing it from the kitchen. Now she'll put him in the dungeon and he'll shake for hours after she lets him out, it's such a frightening place."

"Will you show me where the cellar is?" Josh asked.

"No! I can't," she said with fear in her eyes. "Just go down the stairs and listen for him crying."

"You stay here, Rebecca, while I—"

"I'm going with you," she said, and with determination started off down the stairs.

As they walked through the dimly lit walkway, they heard the pitiful cry of a small child. They walked into the room and shocked a tall, angular woman.

"What are you doing down here? You are not allowed to be here. Go back upstairs at once," she demanded angrily.

The sound of a muffled cry came from behind a grimy door, and Josh strode angrily to the door, jerked it open, reached in, and lifted a small boy from the dark, steaming sweat hole.

"You will pay for this, Lady. I will see that this is reported to the authorities at once." He clasped the grimy, shaking child to his chest, took Rebecca's hand, and rushed back up the stairs before he was tempted to attack the evil woman.

She hurried after the couple with fear in her heart. One thing she didn't need was authorities to prowl around. She had too much to hide. When they reached the front of the house the woman demanded, "Mr. Holt, let me have the boy and we will get to your business."

"Right now this boy is my business. Take us to your office where we can talk," demanded the angry Josh. He still held the sobbing boy to his chest.

She escorted them into her office and took a seat behind her cluttered desk. She appeared to get her spunk back, but just as she started to speak, Josh interrupted. "Who is this child?"

"That is none of your business, Mr. Holt," she replied, haughtily.

"Well, I'm making it my business! What is his name?"

"Jimmy Swanigan," she replied stiffly.

"Does he have brothers and sisters here?"

"No. He was only a few weeks old when he was left here. No one will adopt him because he has a limp. He is three years old now."

Josh stood up and placed the boy on Rebecca's lap. The youngster had almost stopped shaking and looked around with questioning eyes at the strangers. Josh took the papers from his pocket that Mr. Jamison had given him the night before. Laying them on the desk in front of the woman he said, "Here are the adoption papers for Rachael and Levi Smith. They have been staying with us. All you need to do is sign them and we will be on our way."

"I'm afraid it's not that simple. It will have to go before the adoption board and they meet only once a month," she remarked smugly. "You will have to leave the children here and come back in June. If the board approves the adoption you can take them then."

"I'm sorry to disappoint you, Miss McCleese, but I am a little better informed than you think. I know the board meets tomorrow, and you can bet I'll be here. And my children are not spending one night in this hole."

"But the meeting was called off," she said. She didn't inform him that it was canceled because there were no cases pending.

"I believe Mr. Jordan, the bank president, is chairman of the board. I will just walk down and talk to him and see that it is rescheduled. While I am gone you can fill out the adoption papers for Jimmy Swanigan, also. We are taking him with us to the hotel and we will bring him back with the other children tomorrow." He glanced at the shocked Rebecca as he stood up to leave.

"Now just a minute!" the headmistress replied through clenched teeth. "This has gone far enough. You will not leave with that boy and you—"

"Just you watch me, Miss McCleese," he said as he picked up the small, smiling boy. He slipped his arm around Rebecca and walked defiantly out the door and down the street toward the bank.

Mr. Jordan was a fine Christian man, and he listened attentively as Josh told him the situation. He had long suspected the mistreatment of the orphans under the care of Miss McCleese, but hadn't been able to obtain any proof. He assured the Holts that the meeting would take place tomorrow and that there would be no trouble for them to get adoption papers for all three children by tomorrow afternoon. He silently applauded the action Josh had taken to rescue the boy and standing up to "Battle-axe McCleese."

As they stood on the sidewalk in front of the bank, Josh let out a long sigh, releasing the tension that had built up inside him over the last hour. "Oh, Rebecca, what have I done to you? I didn't even ask you if it was all right." He looked at the dirty little boy in his arms and then into her eyes.

"Josh, if you hadn't taken the situation into your own hands, I would have myself. There is no way I could have left him there. Now let's buy him some clothes and then get back to the children."

Josh blinked back the tears that threatened to escape, and they started toward the nearest clothing store.

"Mister, I'm too big for you to carry," said the boy, uttering his first words. "I can walk just fine if you let me down."

With a smile, Josh set him down. He took the boy's grubby little hand in his big strong one and continued down the walk. Josh hid his dismay at the boy's limp. Rebecca reached down and took Jimmy's other hand and with understanding, smiled at her husband. They bought Jimmy two complete outfits and a pair of shoes and returned to the hotel. Josh walked over to the desk and asked that a tub and water be brought to their room. When they walked into the room, Rachael and Levi rushed to meet them, but stopped short at the sight of the boy.

"Children, this is Jimmy. He will be going home with us to live," Josh said, smiling down at Jimmy. Suddenly Levi raced from the room and down the hall. Josh went after him and caught the sobbing boy as he started down the stairs.

"Levi, what is wrong with you?" asked the astounded Josh.

"I didn't know you would find a little boy you liked better than me, or I'd have stayed home," he cried, trying to get free from Josh's grip.

"Son, he's not here to take your place," said Josh, trying to control his tears. "He is just another little boy who needs a home and plenty of love. I have enough love for a dozen little boys like you, but you will always hold a special place in my heart, because you were my first little boy. Will you try to love him?"

"I suppose so!" Levi grinned. "Just as long as I don't have to share my puppy."

"We must always share with others less fortunate than ourselves, but I think we can find him a puppy of his own when we get home."

He climbed on Josh's back, and they galloped back to the room with Levi squealing in delight. Josh smiled at Rebecca to let her know that everything was fine.

By the time Jimmy had taken his bath and dressed in his new clothes, he and Levi were the best of friends. With the dirt and grime washed off and his hair shampooed, they found that he was a pale child with platinum blond hair and icy blue eyes.

They all walked down the street to get supper, and Josh and Rebecca thanked the Lord for the fine family he had given them.

Everything went smoothly at the hearing the next day. By late afternoon they were headed home. Mr. Jordan had privately taken Josh's statement about the deplorable conditions at the home and had assured him that Miss McCleese would be replaced immediately. Josh, Rebecca, and the children dozed as the train rumbled northward to Longmont.

Chapter Twenty-Three

> *Lo, children are an heritage of the Lord: and the fruit of the womb is his reward.*
>
> Psalm 127:3

Rebecca trudged slowly up the stairs. The child lay heavy in her womb and caused her back to ache continually. She seemed to wake up in the mornings as tired as when she went to bed. The June air was muggy and caused rivulets of perspiration to creep down her spine.

Matthew and his family would arrive in three days, and she felt rushed to get the upstairs rooms ready for them. Rachael had to spend more of her time watching over the two boys, which left most of the cooking and housework to Rebecca. Jimmy needed more care than Levi did since he was younger, but what he lacked in age he made up for in mischievousness. Instead of entertaining each other, as she had hoped, they seemed to be able to think of more things to get into.

Rebecca had the large bedroom that overlooked the orchard ready for Matthew and Hannah. The walnut trundle bed seemed to reign in the room and was ideal, since she was sure five-year-old Melinda still slept in the room with her parents. The smaller room was ready for Martin.

She had asked Rachael if she would like to share the other bedroom with Drucilla, leaving the two small boys to share the room downstairs. Her excitement was evident as she moved her belongings to her new domain. All through her childhood she had never had a close friend her own age. The mothers of her school friends would never let their daughters come around because of her father's drinking. Besides, he saw that she had so many chores in the evenings that she fell into bed exhausted at night.

The girls' bedroom was in the front part of the house overlooking the meadow. The limbs of a huge tree in the yard sheltered the room from the hot evening sun. Rebecca had made a comforter and dust ruffle from lavender-flowered chintz. She hoped she could finish the ruffled curtains this morning, and then the room would be ready. She smoothed the covers on the maple bed. On the high headboard were oak leaves and acorns carved across the top. Rachael had hung her clothes in the big maple wardrobe and enjoyed her privacy from the two young rascals.

When the curtains were finished, Rebecca slowly descended the stairs, went into her room, and stretched out across her bed. Her weary body cried for a few minutes' rest before she started supper.

She woke up with a start. She realized the sun was setting, and she didn't have supper ready. Then the aroma of food drifted under the closed bedroom door, causing her to rush clumsily out of her room. The family was all sitting around the table enjoying the meal Rachael had prepared.

"Rachael, why didn't you wake me?" she said, ashamed for sleeping the afternoon away. "I only meant to rest a few minutes."

"We thought you needed the sleep," said Josh, smiling as she waddled across the room. "I shut the door and took the boys out to play while Rachael fixed supper. Come sit down and I'll fix you a plate."

"I'm so ashamed," she said, looking around at her family. "It won't be long until I'm back to normal and can take care of you all."

Later that night as she lay with her head cradled on Josh's arm, he told her of the talk he had had with little Jimmy. The child had never been taught to consider others' feelings and had caused Levi to come crying to him several times the last week.

"He has had so much punishment and so little love that all he knows is how to cause pain," said Josh. "Yesterday, he tied the tails of two little kittens together with twine and then threw the kittens over the fence. They just about clawed themselves to pieces before I could get them down. When he realized how bad they were hurt, he cried and cried. He has never been taught anything about God, so we must start from the beginning and teach him right from wrong. I've decided to start taking him with me when I go out to work and teach him as we work together. After the baby is born and you get back on your feet, then you can teach him about a mother's love."

"But won't Levi feel left out if you spend so much time with Jimmy?" she asked with concern, propping herself up on her elbow.

"I explained it to him and he seemed to understand. He said Jimmy caused him to do too many mean things, but I explained to him that he was responsible for his own actions, that he didn't have to do everything Jimmy suggested," Josh said with a chuckle.

"I just pray that Matthew's children and ours will get along," she said, as she snuggled back into his arms. "We sure will have a houseful."

"The only one I'm concerned about is Dru. Matt said he was having some trouble with her. Since she started in that girls' school, she was acting kind of uppity. She is also very boy-crazy."

"I had hoped Rachael and she could become good friends, but if she's like that maybe they should have separate rooms."

"Don't worry about our girl. She knows right from wrong and has shown a loving heart and concern for others, just like her young mother."

"You know, I am only ten years older than she is, but I feel a hundred," she said with a laugh.

With a twinkle in his eyes, he responded, "I'm six years older than you, but I feel like a sixteen-year old."

"Oh, you!" she said, giving him a loving jab in the ribs. "If you had to carry a huge watermelon around in your apron all day, you wouldn't feel so spry, either."

Rebecca lay quietly for a while, and then said, "Is Dru as pretty as our Rachael?"

"Now, Honey, you know we mustn't judge people by their outward appearances, but what's inside. They will get along fine, as long as Dru stays away from Brent."

"Brent? What do you mean?" she questioned.

"Don't tell me you haven't noticed the sheep eyes they have been casting at each other. Especially since we came back from Denver."

"But she's just a child! You keep that cowpoke of yours away from my girl," she said angrily.

"Now calm down. You have to realize we won't have that girl for long. She is too pretty and the girls get married young out here. Now let's get some sleep," he said, giving her a kiss on her worried brow.

———◆◆———

Rebecca sat in the porch swing and watched up the road as she gently pushed with her slightly swollen foot. It was early in the day, and yet it seemed to be a hundred degrees already. Rachael had gone with Josh to pick up his brother and family at the station, and Dave was keeping an eye on the boys while they were gone so she would be rested when the company arrived.

Little Jimmy had been a changed boy since Josh

had talked to him. He had stayed by Josh's side while he worked, absorbing his teaching like a sponge. He was learning to love his new family and to realize that they corrected him only because they loved him.

The last couple of days Rebecca had spent the cool mornings baking to save time in preparing meals later in the week. The pie safe was full of fruit pies with tender crusts. Two stone crocks were full of her delicious oatmeal raisin cookies. The children could enjoy them with a tall glass of cold milk. A honey-glazed ham was baked and sliced, ready to devour between slices of her freshly baked bread.

Rebecca watched with eagerness, and she soon spied the wagon coming down the road. It was piled high with trunks, and the passengers were squeezed in among them wherever they could find room. She walked slowly to the gate to greet them as the wagon pulled up in front of the house.

"Rebecca," shouted Matt. He jumped from the wagon and gave her a hug, "What has this lunk-head brother of mine done to you! He told us you had three children and another on the way." With a shake of his head, he continued, "He always did like to stay one step ahead of me. Hannah, come meet this little jewel I found for Josh," he said with a laugh.

Hannah jumped from the wagon like a sparrow bird. Fluttering over to Rebecca, she gathered her into her arms as if she had always known her. "Oh, I am so glad to finally meet you. Matt has told me so much about you. I can't believe he sent you out here to face that brother of his all alone." The small, petite woman with mousy brown hair started toward the house, her arm around Rebecca, chattering all the way. The rest of the family followed.

Rachael went to the icebox for a pitcher of iced tea and poured everyone a frosty glass. Drucilla stood just inside the door with a haughty look on her face as she watched Rachael serving the drinks. Her beauty, complimented by blond hair, rosy cheeks, and bright blue eyes, was marred by the look of contempt on her face. Rebecca gave her a hug. *This girl will have a hard time adapting to the West.*

Josh held his little niece, Melinda, in his arms, and she looked timidly at the uncle who was a stranger to her. She had dark brown hair and dark-lashed hazel eyes which she got from her father. Martin was a slender boy with his mother's fine features and coloring.

While the men took the trunks to the rooms, Hannah helped Rebecca put a quick lunch on the table. As Hannah watched Rebecca slowly maneuvering around the kitchen, she remarked, "That baby will be here soon. I guess you have everything ready, don't you?"

"Yes, I'm ready, but I still have a couple of weeks to go," she said, holding her back while she carried a pie to the table.

"Honey, you won't wait that long. I say it will be here before very many days. Looks like we arrived just in time," she said with a laugh.

<hr>

Rebecca woke during the night with pains in her lower back. She tried to get comfortable, but the pain gradually moved to her abdomen, and she knew that her labor had started. She slipped out of bed and sat in a rocker by the window. As she gazed at the moonlit meadow, she deliberated over the news that Matt had brought back from the East. The judge in Morgantown had ruled that she would receive her uncle's entire estate, considering that George left no heir. She was satisfied with her life the way it was, and the inheritance was an unwanted burden. *Oh, God, show me what I should do. Guide me in making my decision.*

She dozed fitfully throughout the early morning hours, her rest disturbed with reoccurring dreams. She relived their visit to Denver where they had found Jimmy. The dream evolved to the point that she brought the entire group of children home with her. Hundreds of children were everywhere—hanging out the windows, romping in the barns, splashing in the stream. Hungry! Always hungry! She had to feed the children!

She awoke with a start. *What a strange dream,* she mused. She watched as the sky turned from black to pale gray and then take on a pinkish glow. She realized the pains signaled the real thing, and she gently woke Josh.

"Josh, it's time," she said, running her hand through his rumpled hair.

He dressed hurriedly and rushed to the bunk-house, aroused Charlie, and sent him after the midwife, then hurried back to her side. When the woman arrived, Hannah realized what was going on and quietly came downstairs and put on a pot of coffee.

Later, when the children woke up, she fed them breakfast and sent them outside to play. Charlie volunteered to keep an eye on them. Rachael had left Dru asleep in bed, and she now paced nervously through the house.

Josh lovingly sat by Rebecca's side throughout the morning. He held her hand and wiped her forehead with a cool cloth. She told him of her dream, and seeing his worried expression, she laughed, then said, "It was just a dream, Josh! As much as I love children, even *I* couldn't manage a hundred," she chuckled. Then a solemn expression covered her face. "They were hungry, Josh, and I couldn't fix enough to feed them all," she mumbled as she drifted off to sleep.

The pains were closer, and she tried to rest between contractions. "Josh," she whispered, after a laborious pain, "We can turn Uncle Hess's house into a private orphanage! We will sell the business and use the money to finance the orphanage. I'm sure Agnes Riley would be delighted to oversee the running of the home." A light of eagerness shone in her eyes as she continued. "I want it to be like a real home, not a workhouse. I want a couple that will be mother and father to the children, people they can look up to and depend on. The house can shelter about twenty-five children easy. I can, oh…" she moaned as another contraction almost took her breath away.

"Honey, I think we should concentrate on bringing our child into the world," said Josh with a gentle smile, "then we can take care of the rest of the children in the world later."

Just before noon, the midwife sent Josh out and asked Hannah to come in and assist her. It wasn't long before Josh heard a lusty cry come from the bedroom. With a grin he went to the door where Hannah met him, saying, "Here is your son, Josh."

Holding back the blanket, he gazed with awe at the tiny bundle of humanity. Its healthy cry let Josh know his son was fine. He gently took him in his arms and as Josh talked, the baby hushed instantly, as if he knew his father's voice. As he and Rachael admired the tiny baby, Hannah once again came to the door.

"And here is your daughter, Josh," she said with a grin. "You have twins!"

Josh looked up with shock. "Two? We have two?" he said, looking at Hannah in disbelief. Hannah gently placed the baby in his other arm. As he turned, Matt walked in. Seeing the big grin on Josh's face and the two bundles, he said, "I'm telling you, boy, you just don't know when to quit, do you?"

With a look of amazement still on his face, Josh carried the babies to Rebecca and laid them in her arms, then gently kissed her brow. "Thank you, dear wife, for these gifts you have given me. I will cherish them, protect them, and love them all their lives. I think this little girl should be named after your mother."

"Susan," whispered the tired Rebecca. "Susan

Abigail. We will call her Abby. And our son will be named Joshua, after his father."

"Joshua Clayton, after his father and grandfather," added Josh, placing his finger in the small hand of his son. "Clayton was my father's name."

"That's a nice name. We can call him Clay. Abby and Clay," smiled the exhausted mother as she drifted off to sleep.

As Josh sat by the bed and admired the two dark-haired babies lying in the arms of his beautiful wife, he bowed his head and began to pray. "Oh, Lord, what a responsibility you have laid upon my shoulders. Lord, help me to bring them up in nurture and admonition of you. May I always set a good example for them to see and not be ashamed for them to follow in my footsteps. Be with this dear mother of my children and keep us together in love, always serving you and putting you first. Thank you for the other children you have entrusted to us, and may we always love them as our own, and teach them your ways. Lord, we again thank you for your many blessings; help us to accept your will in our lives. Amen."

Donna Connelly Stephens lives near Grayson in eastern Kentucky with her husband, Gary. She belongs to Appalachian Heritage Writers, where she has entered their annual short story contest and placed among the winners. She is retired from a managing position at a non-profit organization, Good Samaritans of Carter County, where she worked for ten years. Donna is active in her church where she has been a faithful member for many years. She got the inspiration for her novel from a dream she had.